WOMEN
TALKING

"*Women Talking* is an astonishment, a volcano of a novel with slowly and furiously mounting pressures of anguish and love and rage. No other book I've read in the past year has spoken so lucidly about our current moment, and yet none has felt as timeless; the always-wondrous Miriam Toews has written a book as close to a Greek tragedy as a contemporary Western novelist can come."
—Lauren Groff, author of *Fates and Furies* and *Florida*

"Miriam Toews's *Women Talking* is a flawless, ferocious work of art . . . [An] illuminating quest to comprehend the most vital contours of the human experience: what is agency, what is meaning, what is justice, what is love. This is the kind of novel that changes you. Get ready."
—Laura van den Berg, author of *The Third Hotel*

"Miriam Toews has written a modern classic . . . real and warm and terrifying . . . It's a perfect work of art."
—Catherine Lacey, author of *The Answers* and *Nobody is Ever Missing*

"In the crucible of [Toews'] genius, tears and laughter are ground into some magical elixir that seems like the essence of life . . . [She] is working near the emotional territory of Lorrie Moore, where humor is a bulwark against despair." —Ron Charles, *The Washington Post*

"[A] brilliant writer . . . I want to call her a Canadian Lorrie Moore, but the truth is that Toews is truly distinct, hilarious even when she's dealing with the most heartbreaking and bleak of subjects." —Chloe Schama, *New Republic*

"With wit, warmth and a firm pinch of absurdity, [Toews] powerfully demonstrates the essential role of humour in rendering the unbearable bearable. Her dialogue is fast-paced, vivid, perceptive and frequently hilarious . . . [She] creates battered, loving, whole and original characters who are never less than fascinating company."
—*The Spectator* (UK)

"Underneath [Toews'] stunning writing and outrageous humour are insights—wise and profound—that test the boundaries of human rights and stretch the borders of love." —Naomi Klein

WOMEN
TALKING

ALSO BY MIRIAM TOEWS

Summer of My Amazing Luck (1996)

A Boy of Good Breeding (1998)

Swing Low: A Life (2000)

A Complicated Kindness (2004)

The Flying Troutmans (2008)

Irma Voth (2011)

All My Puny Sorrows (2014)

WOMEN TALKING

A NOVEL

MIRIAM TOEWS

BLOOMSBURY PUBLISHING

NEW YORK · LONDON · OXFORD · NEW DELHI · SYDNEY

BLOOMSBURY PUBLISHING
Bloomsbury Publishing Inc.
1385 Broadway, New York, NY 10018, USA

BLOOMSBURY, BLOOMSBURY PUBLISHING, and the Diana
logo are trademarks of Bloomsbury Publishing Plc

First published in 2018 in Canada by Alfred A. Knopf
First published in the United States 2019

Copyright © Miriam Toews, 2018
Interior images by Willow Dawson

ISBN: HC: 978-1-63557-258-2; HC Indie Bookstore Day
edition: 978-1-63557-424-1;
eBook: 978-1-63557-259-9

Library of Congress Cataloging-in-Publication Data has
been applied for.

2   4   6   8   10   9   7   5   3

Book design by Kelly Hill
Printed and bound in the U.S.A. by Berryville Graphics Inc.,
Berryville, Virginia

To find out more about our authors and books visit
www.bloomsbury.com and sign up for our newsletters.

Bloomsbury books may be purchased for business or promotional
use. For information on bulk purchases please contact Macmillan
Corporate and Premium Sales Department at
specialmarkets@macmillan.com.

For Marj
ricordo le risate

And for Erik
e ancora ridiamo

Between 2005 and 2009, in a remote Mennonite colony in Bolivia named the Manitoba Colony, after the province in Canada, many girls and women would wake in the morning feeling drowsy and in pain, their bodies bruised and bleeding, having been attacked in the night. The attacks were attributed to ghosts and demons. Some members of the community felt the women were being made to suffer by God or Satan as punishment for their sins; many accused the women of lying for attention or to cover up adultery; still others believed everything was the result of wild female imagination.

Eventually, it was revealed that eight men from the colony had been using an animal anesthetic to knock their victims unconscious and rape them. In 2011, these men were convicted in a Bolivian court and received lengthy prison sentences. In 2013, while the convicted men were still in jail, it was reported that similar assaults and other sexual abuses were continuing to take place in the colony.

Women Talking is both a reaction through fiction to these true-life events, and an act of female imagination.

—MT

I.

2.

3.

Pertaining to the meetings in the Molotschna
Colony on June 6 and 7, 2009, as recorded
by August Epp.

Present:

The Loewen women
Greta, the eldest
Mariche, the eldest daughter of Greta
Mejal, a younger daughter of Greta
Autje, a daughter of Mariche

The Friesen women
Agata, the eldest
Ona, the eldest daughter of Agata
Salome, a younger daughter of Agata
Neitje, a niece of Salome

JUNE 6

August Epp, Before the Meeting

MY NAME IS AUGUST EPP—irrelevant for all purposes, other than that I've been appointed the minute-taker for the women's meetings because the women are illiterate and unable to do it themselves. And as these are the minutes, and I the minute-taker (and as I am a schoolteacher and daily instruct my students to do the same), I feel my name should be included at the top of the page together with the date. Ona Friesen, also of the Molotschna Colony, is the woman who asked me if I'd take the minutes—although she didn't use the word "minutes" but rather asked if I would record the meetings and create a document pertaining to them.

We had this conversation last evening, standing on the dirt path between her house and the shed where I've been lodged since returning to the colony seven months ago. (A temporary arrangement, according to Peters, the bishop of Molotschna. "Temporary" could mean any length of time because Peters isn't committed to a conventional understanding of hours and days. We're here, or in heaven, for an eternity, and that's all we need to know. The main houses in the colony are for families, and I'm alone, so it is possible I may always, forever, live in the shed, which doesn't really bother me. It's bigger than a jail cell and large enough for me *and* a horse.)

Ona and I avoided the shadows as we spoke. Once, in mid-sentence, the wind caught her skirt and I felt its hem graze my leg. We side-stepped into the sun, again and then again, as the shadows lengthened, until the sunlight had disappeared and Ona laughed and waved her fist at the setting sun, calling it a traitor, a coward. I grappled with the idea of explaining hemispheres to her, how we are required to share the sun with other parts of the world, that if one were to observe the earth from outer space one could see as many as fifteen sunsets and sunrises in a day—and that perhaps by sharing the sun the world could learn to share everything, learn that everything belonged to everyone! But instead I nodded. Yes, the sun is a coward. Like myself. (I kept silent, too, because it was this tendency of mine to believe, with such exuberance, that we could all share everything that landed me in prison not long ago.) The truth is, I don't have a catchy method of conversing and yet, unfortunately, suffer on a minute-to-minute basis the agony of the unexpressed thought.

Ona laughed again, and her laughter gave me courage, and I wanted to ask if I was a physical reminder of evil to her, and if that was what the colony considered me to be, evil, not because I had been in prison but because of what had happened long ago, before I became incarcerated. Instead, I simply agreed to take the minutes, of course—I have no choice other than to agree because I would do anything for Ona Friesen.

I asked her why the women wanted a record of their meetings if they wouldn't be able to read it? Ona, who is

afflicted with Narfa, or Nervousness—as am I, my name
Epp coming from Aspen, the Trembling Aspen, the tree
with leaves that tremble, the tree that is sometimes called
Women's Tongue because its leaves are in constant
motion—said this in response.

She had seen two animals earlier, very early in the
morning, a squirrel and a rabbit. Ona had watched as
the squirrel charged the rabbit, running full tilt. Just
as the squirrel was about to make contact with the rabbit, the rabbit leapt straight up into the air, two or three
feet. The squirrel, confused, or so Ona thought, then
turned around and charged the rabbit from the other
direction only to encounter empty space once again as
the rabbit, at the very last available second, leapt high
into the air, avoiding contact with the squirrel.

I appreciated this story because it was Ona telling it,
but I didn't understand exactly why she was telling it, or
what it had to do with the minutes.

They were playing! she told me.

Is that so? I asked her.

Ona explained: Perhaps she wasn't meant to have
seen the squirrel and rabbit playing. It had been very
early in the morning, at a time when only Ona was roaming about the colony, her hair too loosely covered, her
dress too untidily hemmed, a suspicious figure—the devil's daughter, as Peters has named her.

But you did see it? I asked her. This secret playing?

Yes, she said, I saw it with my own eyes—which in
that moment, in the telling of the story, were shining
with excitement.

The meetings have been organized hastily by Agata Friesen and Greta Loewen in response to the strange attacks that have haunted the women of Molotschna for the past several years. Since 2005, nearly every girl and woman has been raped by what many in the colony believed to be ghosts, or Satan, supposedly as punishment for their sins. The attacks occurred at night. As their families slept, the girls and women were made unconscious with a spray of the anesthetic used on our farm animals, made from the belladonna plant. The next morning, they would wake up in pain, groggy and often bleeding, and not understand why. Recently, the eight demons responsible for the attacks turned out to be real men from Molotschna, many of whom are the close relatives—brothers, cousins, uncles, nephews—of the women.

I recognized one of the men, barely. He and I had played together when we were children. He knew the names of all the planets, or he made them up anyway. His nickname for me was Froag, which in our language meant "question." I remember that I had wanted to say goodbye to this boy before I left the colony with my parents, but my mother told me that he was having difficulty with his twelve-year-old molars, and had contracted an infection and was confined to his bedroom. I'm not sure, now, if that was true. In any case, neither this boy nor anybody from the colony said goodbye before we left.

The other perpetrators are much younger than me

and hadn't been born, or were babies or toddlers, when I left with my parents, and I have no recollection of them.

Molotschna, like all our colonies, is self-policed. Initially Peters planned to lock the men in a shed (similar to the one I live in) for several decades, but it soon became apparent that the men's lives were in danger. Ona's younger sister, Salome, attacked one of the men with a scythe; and another man was hanged by a group of drunk and angry colonists, male relatives of the victims, from a tree branch by his hands. He died there, forgotten apparently, when the drunk and angry men passed out in the sorghum field next to the tree. After this, Peters, together with the elders, decided to call in the police and have the men arrested— for their own safety, presumably—and taken to the city.

The remaining men of the colony (except for the senile or decrepit, and myself, for humiliating reasons) have gone to the city to post bail for the imprisoned attackers in the hope that they will be able to return to Molotschna while they await trial. And when the perpetrators return, the women of Molotschna will be given the opportunity to forgive these men, thus guaranteeing everyone's place in heaven. If the women don't forgive the men, says Peters, the women will have to leave the colony for the outside world, of which they know nothing. The women have very little time, only two days, to organize their response.

Yesterday, as I have been told by Ona, the women of Molotschna voted. There were three options on the ballot.

1. Do Nothing.
2. Stay and Fight.
3. Leave.

Each option was accompanied by an illustration of its meaning, because the women do not read. (Note: It's not my intention to constantly point out that the women do not read—only when it's necessary to explain certain actions.)

Neitje Friesen, age sixteen, daughter of the late Mina Friesen and now permanent ward of her aunt Salome Friesen (Neitje's father, Balthasar, was sent by Peters to the remote southwest corner of the country some years ago to purchase twelve yearlings and still has not returned), created the illustrations:

"Do Nothing" was accompanied by an empty horizon. (Although I think, but did not say, that this could be used to illustrate the option of leaving as well.)

"Stay and Fight" was accompanied by a drawing of two colony members engaged in a bloody knife duel. (Deemed too violent by the others, but the meaning is clear.)

And the option of "Leave" was accompanied by a drawing of the rear end of a horse. (Again I thought, but did not say, that this implies the women are watching *others* leave.)

The vote was a deadlock between numbers two and three, bloody knife duel and back of horse. The Friesen women, predominantly, want to stay and fight. The Loewens prefer to leave, although evidence of shifting convictions exists in both camps.

There are also some women in Molotschna who voted

to do nothing, to leave things in the hands of the Lord, but they will not be in attendance today. The most vocal of the Do Nothing women is Scarface Janz, a stalwart member of the colony, the resident bonesetter, and also a woman known for having an excellent eye for measuring distances. She once explained to me that, as a Molotschnan, she had everything she wanted; all she had to do was convince herself that she wanted very little.

Ona has informed me that Salome Friesen, a formidable iconoclast, had indicated in yesterday's meeting that "Do Nothing" was in reality not an option, but that allowing women to *vote* for "Do Nothing" would at least be empowering. Mejal (meaning "girl" in Plautdietsch) Loewen, a friendly chain-smoker with two yellow fingertips and what I suspect must be a secret life, had agreed. But, Ona told me, Mejal also pointed out that Salome Friesen had not been anointed as the person who can declare what constitutes reality or what the options are. The other Loewen women had apparently nodded their heads at this while the Friesen women had expressed impatience with quick, dismissive gestures. This type of minor conflict well illustrates the timbre of the debate between the two groups, the Friesens and the Loewens. However, because time is short and the need for a decision urgent, the women of Molotschna have agreed collectively to allow these two families to debate the pros and cons of each option—excluding the Do Nothing option, which most of the women in the colony dismiss as "dummheit"—and to decide which is suitable, and finally to choose how best to implement that option.

A translation note: The women are speaking in
Plautdietsch, or Low German, the only language they
know, and the language spoken by all members of the
Molotschna Colony—although the boys of Molotschna
are now taught rudimentary English in school, and the
men also speak some Spanish. Plautdietsch is an unwritten
medieval language, moribund, a mishmash of German,
Dutch, Pomeranian and Frisian. Very few people in the
world speak Plautdietsch, and everyone who does is
Mennonite. I mention this to explain that before I can
transcribe the minutes of the meetings I must translate
(quickly, in my mind) what the women are saying into
English, so that it may be written down.

And one more note, again irrelevant to the women's
debate, but necessary to explain in this document why I
am able to read, write and understand English: I learned
English in England, where my parents went to live after
being excommunicated by the bishop of Molotschna at
the time, Peters Senior, father of Peters, the current bishop
of Molotschna.

While in my fourth year of university there, I suffered
a nervous breakdown (Narfa) and became involved in certain political activities for which I was eventually expelled
and imprisoned for a period of time. During my imprison-
ment, my mother died. My father had disappeared years
before. I have no siblings because my mother's uterus
was removed following my birth. In short, I had no one
and nothing in England, although I had managed, while
serving time in prison, to complete my teaching degree
through correspondence. In dire straits, homeless and

half-mad—or fully mad—I made a decision to commit suicide.

While researching my various options at the public library nearest the park in which I made my home, I fell asleep. I slept for an extraordinarily long time and was eventually gently nudged by the librarian, who told me it was time for me to leave, the library was closing. Then the librarian, an older woman, noticed that I had been crying and that I appeared dishevelled and distraught. She asked me what was wrong. I told her the truth: I didn't want to live anymore. She offered to buy me supper, and while we were dining at the small restaurant across the street from the library, she asked me where I had come from, what part of the world?

I replied that I came from a part of the world that had been established to be its own world, apart from the world. In a sense, I told her, my people (I remember drawing out the words "my people" ironically, and then immediately feeling ashamed and silently asking to be forgiven) don't exist, or at least are supposed to be seen not to.

And perhaps it doesn't take too long before you believe that you *really* don't exist, she said. Or that your actual corporeal existence is a perversity.

I wasn't sure what she meant and scratched my head furiously, like a dog with ticks.

And after that? she asked.

University, briefly, and then prison, I told her.

Ah, she said, perhaps the two aren't mutually exclusive.

I smiled stupidly. My foray into the world resulted in my removal from the world, I said.

Almost as though you were brought into existence not to exist, she said, laughing.

Singled out to conform. Yes, I said, trying to laugh with her. Born not to be.

I imagined my squalling infant self being removed from my mother's womb and then the womb itself hastily yanked away from her and thrown out a window to prevent any other abominations from occurring—this birth, this boy, his nakedness, her shame, his shame, their shame.

I told the librarian that it was difficult to explain where I was from.

I met a traveller from an antique land, said the librarian, apparently quoting a poet she knew and loved.

Again I wasn't sure what she meant, but I nodded. I explained that I was originally a Mennonite from the Molotschna Colony, and that when I was twelve years old my parents were excommunicated and we moved away, to England. Nobody said goodbye to us, I told the librarian (I live forever with the shame of having said such a piteous thing). For years I believed we were forced to leave Molotschna because I had been caught stealing pears from a farm in the neighbouring colony of Chortiza. In England, where I learned how to read and write, I spelled my name with rocks in a large green field so that God would find me quickly and my punishment would be complete. I also tried to spell the word "confession" with rocks from our garden fence but my mother, Monica, had noticed that the stone wall between our garden and the neighbours' was disappearing. One day she followed me to my green field, along the narrow rut that the wheelbarrow had made in the dirt, and caught me in the act of surrendering myself to God, using the stones from the fence to signal my location, with huge letters. She sat me down on the ground and put her arms around me, and said nothing. After a while, she told me that the fence had to be put back. I asked if I could put the stones back after God had found me and punished me. I was so exhausted from anticipating punishment and I wanted to get it over with. She asked me what I thought God intended to punish me for, and I told her about the pears, and about my thoughts regarding girls, about my drawings, and my desire to win in sports and be strong. How I was vain and competitive and lustful. My mother laughed then, and hugged me again and apologized for laughing. She said that I was a normal boy, I was a child of God—a loving God, in spite of what anybody said—but that the neighbours were perturbed about the disappearing fence and I would have to return the stones.

All this I told to the librarian.

She responded that she could understand why my mother had said what she did, but that if she had been there, if she had been my mother, she would have said something else. She would have told me that I *wasn't* normal—that I was innocent, yes, but that I had an unusually deep need to be forgiven, even though I had done nothing wrong. Most of us, she said, absolve ourselves of responsibility for change by sentimentalizing our pasts. And then we live freely, happily, or if not altogether happily, without tremendous anguish. The librarian laughed. She said that if she had been in that green field with me, she would have helped me to have that feeling of somehow being forgiven.

Forgiven for what, though, exactly? I asked her. Stealing pears, drawing pictures of naked girls?

No, no, said the librarian, forgiven for being alive, for being in the world. For the arrogance and the futility of remaining alive, the ridiculousness of it, the stench of it, the unreasonableness of it. That's your feeling, she added, your internal logic. You've just explained that to me.

She went on to say that, in her opinion, doubt and uncertainty and questioning are inextricably bound together with faith. A rich existence, she said, a way of being in the world, wouldn't you say?

I smiled. I scratched. The world, I said.

What do you remember of Molotschna?

Ona, I said. Ona Friesen.

And I began to tell her about Ona Friesen, a girl my age, the same woman who has now asked me to record the minutes of the meeting.

After a long conversation with the librarian, during which I talked mostly, though not entirely, about Ona—how we had played, how we had clocked the seasons by the tiny lengthening of light, how we had pretended to be rebellious disciples at first misunderstood by our leader, Jesus, and then posthumously hailed as heroes, how we had jousted on horses with fence posts (running full tilt, like knights, like Ona's squirrel and rabbit), how we had kissed, how we'd fought—the librarian suggested that I return to Molotschna, to the place where life had made sense to me, even briefly, even in imaginary play in dying sunlight, and that I ask the bishop (Peters, the younger, who was the same age as my mother) to accept me into the colony as a member. (I did not tell the librarian that this would also mean asking Peters to forgive me the sins of my parents, sins pertaining to the storage of intellectual materials and to the dissemination and propagation of said materials, even though the materials were art books, photographs of paintings that my father had found in the garbage behind a school in the city, and even though he was guilty only of sharing the images with other colony members, as he was unable to read the text.) She also suggested that I offer to teach the Molotschnan boys English, a language they would need in order to conduct business outside the colony. And she said that I should become friends, once again, with Ona Friesen.

I had nothing to lose. I took this advice to heart.

The librarian asked her husband to give me a job driving for his airport limousine service, and although I didn't have a valid driver's licence, I worked for him for three months to make enough money to purchase a ticket to Molotschna. During this time, I slept in the attic of a youth hostel. At night, when it felt as though my head was about to explode, I would will myself to lie as still as possible. Every night, in that hostel, as I lay motionless in my bed, I closed my eyes and heard very faint strains of piano music, heavy chords unaccompanied by voices. One morning I asked the man who cleaned the hostel, and who also slept there, if he had ever heard faint piano music with heavy chords at night. He said no, never. Eventually, I understood that the song I heard at night, when it felt as though my head was about to explode, was the hymn "Great Is Thy Faithfulness," and that I was listening to my own funeral.

Peters, who wears the same tall black boots his own father once wore, or at least similar ones, considered my request for re-admittance into the colony. He finally said he would allow me membership providing I renounced my parents (in spite of one being dead and the other missing) before the elders and was baptized into the church and agreed to teach the boys basic English and simple math in return for shelter (the aforementioned shed) and three meals a day.

I told Peters I would be baptized and I would teach the boys, but that I wouldn't renounce my parents. Peters, unhappy, but desperate to have the boys learn accounting, or perhaps because my appearance unsettled him, as I looked so much like my father, agreed.

When I arrived in the spring of 2008, there were only whispers, fragments of whispers, concerning the mysterious night-time disturbances. Cornelius, one of my students, wrote a poem called "The Washline" in which he described the sheets and garments on his mother's washline as having voices, of speaking with one another, of sending messages to other garments on other washlines. He read the poem to the class and all the boys laughed. The houses are so far apart and there is no electrical light anywhere, inside or out. The houses are small tombs at night.

On my way back to my shed that afternoon I saw the washlines of Molotschna, I saw the women's dresses flapping in the wind and the men's overalls and the linens and the bedding and the towels. I listened carefully but I couldn't make out what they were saying. Perhaps, I now think, because they weren't talking to me. They were talking to each other.

In the year after I arrived, the women described dreams they'd been having, and then eventually, as the pieces fell into place, they came to understand that they were collectively dreaming one dream, and that it wasn't a dream at all.

The women in the Friesen and the Loewen families who have gathered for today's meeting represent three generations each, and all have been repeat victims in the attacks. I've done some simple calculations. Between 2005 and 2009, more than three hundred girls and women of Molotschna were made unconscious and attacked in their own beds. On average, an attack occurred every three or four days.

Finally, Leisl Neustadter forced herself to stay awake night after night until she caught a young man prying open her bedroom window, holding a jug of belladonna spray in one hand. Leisl and her adult daughter wrestled the man to the ground and tied him up with baler twine. Later that morning, Peters was brought to the house to confront this young man, Gerhard Schellenberg, and Gerhard named the other seven men involved in the attacks.

Nearly every female member of the Molotschna Colony has been violated by this group of eight, but most (except for the girls too young to understand these proceedings, and the women, led by Scarface Janz, who have already chosen to exercise the Do Nothing option) have marked an *X* next to their name to indicate that they are content (and many ecstatic) not to attend the meetings about how to respond. Instead, they will contribute to the well-being of the colony by tending to the chores, which are manifold now while the men are away, and which if abandoned for as little as one day will result in mayhem, especially when it comes to the milking and feeding of the animals.

The youngest and speediest women in both the Friesen and Loewen families, Autje and Neitje, have agreed to provide the other women in the colony with oral reports at the end of the day, when all are back in their houses.

Now, in the hayloft of the barn where we have quietly gathered this morning, I wait to do as Ona has asked of me.

JUNE 6

Minutes of the Women Talking

WE BEGIN BY WASHING each other's feet. This takes time. We each wash the feet of the person sitting to our right. The foot-washing was a suggestion made by Agata Friesen (mother of Ona and Salome Friesen). It would be an appropriate symbolic act representing our service to each other, she said, just as Jesus washed the feet of his disciples at the Last Supper, knowing that his hour had come.

Four of the eight women are wearing plastic sandals with white socks, two are wearing sturdy leather shoes, scuffed (and in one case slit open at the side to allow for a growing bunion), with white socks, and the other two, the youngest, are wearing torn canvas running shoes, also with white socks. Socks are always worn by the women of Molotschna, and it appears to be a rule that the top of the socks must always reach the bottom hem of the dress.

The two youngest women, Autje and Neitje, the ones wearing running shoes, have rolled their socks down rebelliously (and stylishly) into little doughnuts that encircle their ankles. On them, a swatch of bare skin, several inches of skin, is visible between the rolled sock and the dress hem, and insect bites (probably black fly and chigger) dot the skin. Faint scars, from rope burns or from cuts, are also visible on the exposed parts of these women. Autje and Neitje, both sixteen, are having difficulty keeping straight faces during the foot-washing, murmuring to each other that it's ticklish, and coming close to erupting in giggles when attempting to say *God bless you* to each other, in solemn voices, as their mothers, aunts and grandmothers have done following each washing.

Greta Loewen, the eldest of the Loewen women (although she was born a Penner) begins. She exudes a deep, melancholic dignity as she speaks of her horses, Ruth and Cheryl. She describes how when Ruth (who is blind in one eye and must always be harnessed to the left of Cheryl) and Cheryl are frightened by one or more of Dueck's Rottweilers on the mile road that leads to church, their initial instinct is to bolt.

We have seen it happen, she says. (After these short, declarative sentences Greta has a habit of lifting her arms, dipping her head and widening her eyes as if to say, This is a fact, are you challenging me?)

Greta explains that these horses, upon being startled by Dueck's stupid dog, don't organize meetings to determine their next course of action. They run. And by so doing, evade the dog and potential harm.

Agata Friesen, the eldest of the Friesen women (although born a Loewen) laughs, as she does frequently and charmingly, and agrees. But Greta, she states, we are not animals.

Greta replies that we have been preyed upon like animals; perhaps we should respond in kind.

Do you mean we should run away? asks Ona.

Or kill our attackers? asks Salome.

(Mariche, Greta's eldest, until now silent, makes a soft scoffing sound.)

Note: As I have mentioned, Salome Friesen *did* assault the attackers with a scythe, whereupon the attackers were promptly rescued by Peters and the elders, and the police were called to the colony. At no other time in the history of Molotschna have the police been called. The attackers were brought to the city for their own protection.

Salome has since asked Peters and the elders to be forgiven for that indiscretion, but even so, her rage is barely suppressed, vesuvian. Her eyes are never still. Even if, one day, she runs out of words like a woman is said to run out of "eggs," I believe that Salome will be able to communicate and to give life, fearsome life, to every emotion stemming from each injustice she perceives. There is no Inward Eye in Salome, no bliss of solitude. She doesn't wander. And she is not lonely. Her niece Neitje, used to the gentler stylings of her late mother, Mina, but now in Salome's care, keeps her distance. Neitje draws and draws, perhaps to balance the wild, lava-like outpouring of her aunt's words with solid, silent lines on paper. (In addition to her drawing skills, I have been told that Neitje is also Molotschna's reigning champion of knowing how much of anything—flour, salt, lard—will fit into any given container so that nothing and no extra space is ever wasted.)

Agata Friesen, unfazed by Salome's outbursts (she has already referred to Ecclesiastes to describe Salome's temper as nothing new under the sun, as the wind blows from the north, as all streams lead to the sea, etc. To which Salome responded that her opinions should not be slotted under hoary Old Testament headings, please, and wasn't it preposterous that the women should compare themselves to animals, wind, sea, etc.? Isn't there a human precedent, some person in whom we can see ourselves reflected back to ourselves? To which Mejal, lighting up a smoke, responded, Yes, I'd like that, too, but what humans? Where?), states that in her lifetime she has seen horses, perhaps not Ruth or Cheryl, fair enough—in deference to Greta and her high regard for her horses—but others who, when charged by a dog or coyote or jaguar, have attempted to confront the animal and/or to stomp the creature to death. So it isn't always the case that animals flee their attackers.

Greta acknowledges this: Yes, she has seen similar behaviour in animals. She begins once again to talk of Ruth and Cheryl, but her anecdote is cut short by Agata.

Agata tells the group she has her own animal story, also featuring Dueck's Rottweiler. She speaks quickly, often inserting asides and non sequiturs in a hushed, theatrical voice.

I am not able to hear or keep up with every detail, but I'll attempt here to tell the story in her voice, and with as much accuracy as I am able.

Dueck had raccoons in his yard that he hated for a long time, and when the fattest raccoon suddenly had six babies, it was all that Dueck could stand. He tore his hair out. He told his Rottweiler to go kill them, and away the dog went, and the mother raccoon was surprised and tried to save her babies and get away from the dog, but the dog killed three of the babies and the mother raccoon could only save the other three. She took those babies and left Dueck's yard. Dueck was fairly happy about that. He drank his instant coffee, and thought, praise be to God, no more raccoons. But a few days later, he looked into his yard and saw the three baby raccoons sitting there, and he became angry once again. He told his Rottweiler again to attack and kill them. But this time the mother raccoon was waiting for the dog, and when he came running at the babies she jumped on him from a tree and bit into his neck and his stomach and then, with every muscle in her body straining, dragged him into the bushes. Dueck was so mad, and also sad. He wanted his dog back. He went into the bushes to find the dog, but he couldn't, even after two days of searching. He cried. When he came back home he walked despondently to his door and there lay one leg from his dog, and also the dog's head. With empty eye sockets.

The reaction to Agata's story is mixed. Greta lifts her hands over her head and asks the other women: What are we supposed to make of this? Are we to leave our most vulnerable colony members exposed to further attack in order to lure the men to their deaths so they can be dismembered and delivered in parts to the doorstep of Peters, the bishop of our colony?

What the story proves is that animals can fight back *and* they can run away, Agata says. And so it doesn't matter whether we are animals or not, or whether we have been treated like animals or not, or even if we can know the answer to that one way or the other. (She inhales all possible oxygen into her lungs and then releases it with the next sentence.) Either way, it's a waste of time to try to establish whether we are animals or not, when the men will soon be returning from the city.

Mariche Loewen raises her hand. One of her fingers, her left index, has been bitten off at the knuckle. It is half as long as the middle finger next to it. She asserts that in her opinion, the more important question to ask is not whether the women are animals, but rather, should the women avenge the harm perpetrated against them? Or should they instead forgive the men and by doing so be allowed to enter the gates of heaven? We will be forced to leave the colony, she says, if we don't forgive the men and/or accept their apologies, and through the process of this excommunication we will forfeit our place in heaven. (Note: This is true, I know, according to the rules of Molotschna.)

Mariche sees me looking at her and asks if I'm writing this down.

I nod, yes, I am.

Satisfied, Mariche asks the others a question about the rapture. How will the Lord, when He arrives, find all the women if we aren't in Molotschna?

Salome cuts her off, disdainful. In a mocking voice, she begins to explain that if Jesus is able to return to life, live for thousands of years and then drop down to earth from heaven to scoop up his supporters, surely he'd also be able to locate a few women who—

But now Salome is silenced by her mother, Agata, with a quick gesture. We will return to that question later, Agata says kindly.

Mariche's eyes dart around the room, perhaps searching for kinship on this subject, someone to share her fears. The others look away.

Salome is muttering: But if we're animals, or even animal-like, perhaps there's no chance anyway of entering the gates of heaven—(she stands up and goes to the window)—unless animals are permitted. Although that doesn't make sense because animals provide food and labour, and we will require neither of those things in heaven. So perhaps, after all, Mennonite women will not be allowed into heaven because we fall into the category of animals, who will not be needed up there, where it's always *lalalalala* . . . She ends her sentence in song syllables.

The other women, except Ona Friesen, her sister, ignore her. Ona smiles slightly, encouragingly, approvingly, although it's also a smile that could serve as firm punctuation to Salome's statement—that is, a silent request to end it. (The Friesen women have developed a mostly effective system of gestures and facial expressions to quiet Salome.)

Ona begins to speak now. She is reminded of a dream she had two nights ago: She found a hard candy in the dirt behind her home and had picked it up and taken it into her kitchen, planning to wash it and eat it. Before she could wash it, she was accosted by a very large two-hundred-pound pig. She screamed, Get that pig off me! But it had her pinned against the wall.

That's ridiculous, says Mariche. We don't have hard candy in Molotschna.

Agata reaches over to touch Ona's hand. You can tell us your dreams later, she says. When the meeting is over.

Several of the women speak up now, saying they are not able to forgive the men.

Precisely, says Mariche. She speaks succinctly, sure of herself again. Yet we want to enter the gates of heaven when we die.

None of the women argue that point.

Mariche goes on to state that we should then not put ourselves in an unfortunate position, where we are forced to choose between forgiveness and eternal life.

What position would that be? asks Ona Friesen.

That position would be staying behind to fight, Mariche says. Because the fight would be lost to the men, and we would be guilty of the sin of rebellion and of betraying our vow of pacifism and would finally be plunged deeper into submissiveness and vulnerability. Furthermore, we would be forced to forgive the men anyway, if we wanted God to forgive us and to allow us into His kingdom.

But is forgiveness that is coerced true forgiveness? asks Ona Friesen. And isn't the lie of pretending to forgive with words but not with one's heart a more grievous sin than to simply not forgive? Can't there be a category of forgiveness that is up to God alone, a category that includes the perpetration of violence upon one's children, an act so impossible for a parent to forgive that God, in His wisdom, would take exclusively upon Himself the responsibility for such forgiveness?

Do you mean that God would allow the parent of the violated child to harbour just a tiny bit of hatred inside her heart? asks Salome. Just in order to survive?

A tiny bit of hate? asks Mejal. That's ridiculous. And from tiny seeds of hate bigger—

It's not ridiculous, says Salome. A very small amount of hate is a necessary ingredient to life.

To life? says Mejal. You mean to waging war. I've noticed how you come alive in the act of killing.

Salome rolls her eyes. Not war; survival. And let's not call it hate—

Oh, you'd prefer to call it an "ingredient," says Mejal.

When I must kill pigs, I hit the runts harder, says Salome, because it's more humane to kill them with one swift blow than to torture them with tepid hacks, which your system . . .

I wasn't talking about killing pigs, says Mejal.

During this exchange, Mariche's daughter Autje has begun swinging from a rafter, a human pendulum, kicking at bales mid-swing and loosening the straw, a piece of which has landed in Salome's hair. Mejal looks up, tells Autje to behave herself, can't she hear the rafter creaking, does she want the roof to cave in? (I muse that perhaps she does.)

Mejal reaches for her pouch of tobacco but doesn't roll a smoke, simply rests her hand lightly on the pouch as though it were a gear shift in an idling getaway car, and she is waiting, knowing it is there when she needs it because her hand is on it.

Salome doesn't know about the straw in her hair. It sits above her ear, nestled in that space, like a librarian's No. 2 pencil.

After a small silence, Greta returns to Ona's question. Perhaps, yes, such a category exists, she says slowly. Except there's no Biblical precedent for this type of God-only forgiveness.

A brief observation about Ona Friesen: Ona is distinctive amongst these women for having her hair pulled back loosely rather than with the blunt force of a seemingly primitive tool. She is perceived by most of the colonists to have a gentle disposition and an inability to function in the real world (although in Molotschna that argument is a red herring). She is a spinster. And she is afforded a type of liberty to speak her mind because her thoughts and words are perceived as meaningless, although this didn't prevent her from being attacked repeatedly. She was a reliable target because she slept alone in a room rather than with a husband, which she doesn't have. Or want, it seems.

Earlier she had stated: When we have liberated ourselves, we will have to ask ourselves who we are. Now she asks: Is it accurate to say that at this moment we women are asking ourselves what our priority is, and what is right—to protect our children or to enter the kingdom of heaven?

Mejal Loewen says, No. That is not accurate. That is an exaggeration of what is truly being discussed. (Her hand still resting intimately on the pouch of tobacco.)

What, then, is truly being discussed? Ona asks.

Agata Friesen, Ona's mother (and Mejal's aunt), responds. We will burn that bridge when we come to it, she says (intentionally using this English expression incorrectly in order to leaven the proceedings). And Ona, indulgent of her mother, as she is of her sister, is content to let it be.

I must record here that Greta Loewen's eyes are opening and closing, and often tears roll down her cheeks. She is not crying, she says, she is moisturizing. Neitje Friesen and Autje Loewen (who has stopped swinging from the rafter) are restless in their chairs and are half-heartedly playing some type of clapping game, their hands hidden beneath the table.

I suggest that we adjourn for a short period, and the women approve.

Agata Friesen suggests that we sing a hymn before dispersing and the others (minus Neitje and Autje, who appear appalled at the thought of collective singing) agree. The women join hands and sing "Work, for the Night Is Coming." Ona Friesen harmonizes, spell-bindingly. The first verse of the hymn is as follows:

> *Work, for the night is coming,*
> *Work through the morning hours;*
> *Work while the dew is sparkling,*
> *Work 'mid springing flowers;*
> *Work when the day grows brighter,*
> *Work in the glowing sun;*
> *Work, for the night is coming,*
> *When man's work is done.*

The women continue to sing verses two and three, and Neitje and Autje crumple in defeat.

Greta Loewen pats Autje's hand. *Steady on.* The knuckles on Greta's hand stand out like knobs, like desert buttes on a cracked surface. Her false teeth are too big for her mouth, and painful. She removes them and sets them down on the plywood. They were given to her by a well-meaning traveller who had come to Molotschna with a first aid kit after hearing about the attacks on the women.

When Greta had cried out, the attacker covered her mouth with such force that nearly all her teeth, which were old and fragile, were crushed to dust. The traveller who gave Greta her false teeth was escorted out of Molotschna by Peters, who then forbade outside helpers from entering the colony.

The singing has ended. The women disperse.

Note: Salome Friesen left earlier, exasperated, after Ona asked if the women were discussing what was right, to protect the children or to enter the kingdom of heaven, and if it wasn't possible to do both. I hadn't the time then to write down the details of her departure.

Agata laughed gently when Salome left, telling the others that her daughter would be back, not to worry, let her blow off steam, let her be, let her check on her children, Miep and Aaron. That would settle her.

When it comes to her children, Salome's patience and

tolerance know no bounds, but Salome's reputation in the colony is that of a fighter, an instigator. She doesn't react calmly to authority and is often engaged in a battle of wills with other colony members over the slightest of things. For example: once she hid the dining hall bell and claimed to have forgotten where she hid it, all because she resented the tone of the clang three "bloody" times a day, and particularly resented the pride that Sarah N. took in ringing the bell incessantly, more than is necessary. (Stop telling me when I must eat! Salome cried.) She also turned Peters' rain barrel upside down during a massive downpour, shrieking that he was too pure to need washing water, wasn't he? Wasn't he!

I find it curious that she hasn't been excommunicated. Are her small acts of rebellion a convenient outlet for Peters, a type of performance that satisfies the colonists' need to assert themselves, and that allows Peters to act with impunity on larger issues?

Another note: As Ona was leaving the loft, I managed to tell her that I liked her dream, the one about the pig. She laughed. I then mustered the courage to tell her a fact.

Did you know, I said to Ona (by now she was climbing down the ladder, still laughing; she was the last to leave the loft), that it's physically impossible for pigs to look up at the sky?

Just then, in that moment, Ona looked up at me from her rung on the ladder.

Like this? she said.

This made *me* laugh. Ona left, satisfied.

She will be the one to look up to the sky, I thought. That is why the pig in her dream had her pinned against the wall. But then I thought, how could that be? How could my interpretation of Ona's dream be accurate when Ona wasn't aware, consciously or not, of the physical limitations of pigs?

In my jail cell (Wandsworth Prison) in England, my cell-mates and I would play games. "What Would You Prefer" was the name of my favourite game. Knowing you were about to die, would you prefer one year, one day, one minute or no time at all to live with that knowledge? The answer is: None of the above.

In jail I once made the mistake of telling my cellmates that the sound of a duck (and also the sight of its round, flat bill) made me happy and provided consolation. There are crimes. And then there are crimes. I have since learned to keep most of my thoughts to myself.

We have reconvened. And I'm embarrassed.

Outside, during our break, I met young Autje at the pump. At first, we were silent. She pumped water vigorously and I stared at the ground.

When she had filled her pail I cleared my throat and mentioned to her that during the war, the Second World War, in Italy for example, specifically in Turin but in many other places as well, civilians would hide in bomb shelters. Often these civilians were murdered, I added, for participating in the Resistance.

Autje slowly crept away backwards, smiling, nodding.

Yes, I said, also nodding and smiling. In these bomb shelters volunteers were needed to power, by riding a bicycle, the generators that provided electricity. When she was swinging from the rafter earlier, with such vigour, it had reminded me of this fact, and of the volunteers who had generated this energy by riding a bicycle. She would be the perfect volunteer to do just that, I told Autje, if we were in a bomb shelter.

Autje asked me, logically, where she would ride the bike *to* if we were in such an enclosed space?

Ah yes, I said. Well, the bike would be stationary.

Autje smiled and seemed to ponder this for a second or two. Then she reminded me that she had to get the water over to the yearlings. First, though, she showed me how she could swing the pail of water around in a complete circle without spilling a drop. I smiled, awkwardly. She ran towards the horses.

I waved stupidly at her back, at the cloud of dust she left in her wake. I stood in the dirt, my shirt-tail flapping, like an absurd flightless bird. Why had I mentioned the Resistance, and that civilians had been murdered for their defiance? It dawned on me that I had suggested she was susceptible to being executed.

I wanted to run after Autje and apologize for scaring her—but that would have scared her even more. Or perhaps my words are as ridiculous to her as they are to me, which is comforting only a little.

Salome has returned, her eyes like asteroids now. Planet-destroying asteroids. (She may not have seen her children. I am afraid to query her directly.)

Since we concluded our first part of the meeting with a hymn, I say to the women, Would it be acceptable if I were to begin our next part with a fact that could act as a metaphor and inspiration?

The women agree, although Mariche frowns and goes to the window to look out as I speak.

I thank the women and begin by reminding them that we Mennonites of Molotschna came to settle this land by way of the Black Sea. Our members had for centuries inhabited the shores of the Black Sea, near Odessa, and had experienced, until we began to be slaughtered, much peace and happiness. I state the fact: The deep waters of the Black Sea do not mix with the upper layers of water that receive oxygen from the atmosphere, making the deep waters anoxic, which means that they do not contain life. Anoxic conditions leave remarkably preserved fossils, and on those fossils the images of soft body parts are visible. But where does that life come from? There are no low or high tides, so the surface of the Black Sea is always calm and serene. Yet underwater there is a river, a mysterious river that scientists believe can sustain life in the bottom part of the Black Sea, the inhospitable part. But these scientists have no way of proving it.

The women's reaction to the inspirational fact is, once again, mixed—with silence being the most common response. Ona Friesen, who is known to appreciate facts, thanks me. When she speaks, Ona ends her sentences with a brisk inhalation of breath, as though she is attempting to take back her words, as though what she has just said has startled her.

Mariche Loewen, who has been standing with her back to us, turns away from the window.

Are you implying, she asks me, that the women should stay in Molotschna rather than leave? That the "upper layers" of the Black Sea represent the men of the colony and the "lower layers" the women who would somehow, mysteriously, thrive in spite of being beneath the severe and lifeless pressure of the men?

I am entirely to blame for this misunderstanding, I say, but I mean only to somehow convey that life and the preservation of life is a possibility even when circumstances appear to be hopeless.

I meant it to be inspirational, I say.

Mariche reminds me that the women had asked me to take the minutes of their meetings only because I was able to translate and to write, and I should not feel obliged to offer inspirational counselling.

Salome Friesen quickly suggests to Mariche that her reaction is inappropriate. Whereupon Mejal Loewen reminds Salome once again that she has not been given special powers to declare what is or isn't appropriate.

Maybe I have been, says Salome.

By whom? asks Mejal. Peters? God?

The surface of Molotschna, like the surface of the Black Sea, is always calm and serene, says Salome. Don't you understand—

So what? interrupts Mejal.

Ona, intent on further examining the mysterious Black Sea scenario, asks, What is soft tissue, exactly?

It's the skin and the flesh and all the connective

material, answers Agata. It's anything that protects the hard tissue, like bones or anything rigid, I suppose.

So, says Mariche, the soft tissue protects the harder tissue, like the tissue that makes bones. The soft tissue is more—what would you call it?—resilient, and yet it decomposes much more quickly in the end. Unless it's preserved in the *mysterious deep waters of the Black Sea*, she adds, separating the words "mysterious deep waters of the Black Sea" from the beginning of the sentence to give them histrionic emphasis. I understand this to be mockery directed at myself.

I smile. I dig my nails into the top of my scalp. I say that soft tissue is often defined by what it is not.

I suppose so, says Agata, but—

And yet, it's stronger in a way, Mariche interrupts, in that it has restorative qualities. Before the end.

Well, says Agata, perhaps, although—

Do you mean death? asks Ona. When you say "the end"?

Mariche makes a gesture: What on earth else would the end be, if not death?

But Mariche, says Greta, physical death is not the end of life.

Autje and Neitje are ignoring the other women now, and engaged in a private conversation of their own. Neitje is nodding, smiling, and glancing in my direction. I wonder, briefly, if Autje is mentioning our water pump conversation to Neitje. Again, predictably, I behave stupidly and nod cautiously to the girls, who instantly look away.

So, says Ona, we women are the soft tissue of Molotschna, if the colony is a body, and—

Or, says Salome, the colony is the Black Sea and we are its "mysterious deep waters." I tried to tell you that.

Mariche laughs and sarcastically asks Salome what, in her divine wisdom, is mysterious about the women of Molotschna? There's more mystery in the skin that forms on top of my morning milk, she says.

Ona acknowledges the mystery of the milk skin, nodding at Mariche, in an attempt, I think, at friendship or solidarity. Kindness. Ona asks me if I wish to bestow upon the women any other inspirational facts.

I rub the top of my head briskly, a simian instinct I picked up in prison. I felt it gave me a slim margin of time to compose my response to a question, a question such as: Epp, motherfucker, are you interested in having your brains smashed in?

The gesture makes Ona laugh.

Yes, I say. Humans shed approximately forty pounds of skin in their lifetime, completely replacing their outer skin every month.

Neitje interrupts. Except for the scars, she says. Can they be replaced with fresh skin? No, says Autje, that's why they're called scars, idiot. The young women laugh, and punch at each other without making contact.

Ona muses that the replacement of their outer skin every month coincides with the replacement of their uterine lining, also every month.

How do you know that? Mariche asks, and Ona looks at me. This is something my mother had told Ona long ago in my mother's secret schoolhouse, which was not a physical place at all, but a discussion that she called "the secret schoolhouse." She held it for girls, during milking, when we were children, Ona and I, before I left Molotschna with my parents.

Mariche glares at me and asks if I had explained things to Ona about her uterine lining.

No, says Ona, not August. August's mother, Monica.

Mariche is silent.

Salome comments that this explanation is probably useful, but shouldn't we move on?

Ona, as if she has not heard Salome, mentions that if my fact is true, the skin they, the women, had during the attacks is gone now, has been replaced. She smiles.

She looks as if she would say more, but now Agata Friesen, sensing Salome's impatience and impending rage, briskly asks if we might put aside the animal/non-animal and forgiveness/non-forgiveness and inspirational/non-inspirational and soft tissue/hard tissue/new skin/old skin debates to concentrate on the matter at hand, which is whether to stay and fight or leave.

The women agree that we should move on.

Meanwhile, Salome has flung her milk pail to the side; it's wobbly and bothering her. Ona gets up, gives Salome her own pail to sit on, and retrieves Salome's wobbly pail for herself.

Once she is sitting again, Ona Friesen continues to consider something said earlier. She mentions that Mariche's use of the word "counselling" has brought to her mind another issue. She requests permission to make one more statement regarding forgiveness.

The women agree. (Although Neitje Friesen's eyes roll in their sockets as her head snaps back and her jaw drops open. Amusing.)

Ona speaks: If it has been decided by the elders and the bishop of Molotschna that we women don't require counselling following these attacks because we weren't conscious when they happened, then what are we obliged, or even able, to forgive? Something that didn't happen? Something that we are unable to understand? And what does that mean more broadly? If we don't know "the world," we won't be corrupted by it? If we don't know that we are imprisoned then we are free?

The teenagers Neitje Friesen and Autje Loewen are now engaged in a contest using body language, attempting to outdo each other to convey their boredom and discomfort. Autje has pretended, for example, to have shot herself in the head by inserting a rifle into her mouth, then slumping over on her milk pail. Neitje has asked plaintively: But are we staying or going? She is resting her head on her arm. Her voice is muffled. Her palm is open and facing upwards as though she is waiting for an answer, or for a cyanide capsule to be placed inside that palm. She has removed her kerchief and I can see one long, thin, very white line running down the centre of her scalp. It is naked skin—called a "parting" by the women.

Greta Loewen sighs heavily. She says that although we may not be animals we have been treated worse than animals, and that in fact Molotschna animals are safer than Molotschna women, and better cared for.

Agata Friesen reminds Greta that, due to issues of time, we have agreed to abandon the question of whether the women are animals or not.

Greta waves aside Agata's reprimand and closes her eyes. She is tapping her false teeth on the plywood.

Mariche interjects: I believe the only solution is to flee.

Oh, but the idea of fleeing has created an uproar amongst the women!

They are talking at once. Still talking at once. Still talking at once.

Ona looks at me. I look at the minutes. From nervousness, because of Ona's glance, I clear my throat—which the women take to be a gesture of impatience on my part, an interruption. They stop talking.

Mariche glares at me.

I stroke my throat as though it's ticklish, the beginning of an illness, perhaps strep like young Aaron's. I haven't meant to interrupt. I am an obstacle to Mariche, and possibly to Salome, who is impatient for other reasons, like a sudden flood, like a chipped hoof. (These are her words, muttered, but they don't translate well.)

Now Salome Friesen asks, aggressively, Is this how we want to teach our daughters to defend themselves—by fleeing?

Mejal Loewen interjects: Not fleeing, but leaving. We're talking about leaving.

Salome Friesen acts as though she hasn't heard Mejal:

Fleeing! I'd rather stand my ground and shoot each man in the heart and bury them in a pit than *flee*, and I'll deal with God's wrath if I have to!

Salome, Ona says gently, please be calm. The Loewens are talking about *leaving* not fleeing. The word "fleeing" was improperly used. Set it aside.

Mariche shakes her head at this, indignant. She apologizes sarcastically for using the incorrect word, a sin so outrageous that Salome with her Olympian airs and almighty mind must take it upon herself to rectify for the sake of all humanity.

Salome strongly objects. She counter-accuses Mariche of being reckless with words. "Leaving" and "fleeing" are two vastly different words, she says, with different meanings and with specific implications.

Autje and Neitje have now begun to take some interest in the proceedings, both stifling giggles. Meanwhile, Greta and Agata wear stern but resigned expressions that speak to years of experience with this type of *opprua* (uproar) from their daughters. Agata's hands are clasped and she is spinning her thumbs around each other. Greta is patting her own head.

Ona Friesen is staring wistfully out of the north-facing window, towards Rembrandt's canola field, towards the hills, and towards the border and a vision of her own making, perhaps.

Mejal Loewen has surreptitiously begun to roll herself a smoke. (Left over from the last one, which she had extinguished, stylishly, by pinching it with her finger and thumb.)

Well, August? says Agata. She is sitting next to me. She has put her arm around my shoulder! What do you make of all this? Do you have an opinion too?

What comes into my head is the story of the Korean poet Ko Un. So I tell the women how he had tried to commit suicide four times, once by pouring poison into one of his ears. He survived but destroyed his eardrum. The other eardrum had been damaged when he was a political prisoner and was tortured. During the Korean War he was forced to carry dead bodies on his back. Then he became a monk for ten years.

The women have stopped arguing and are listening to my story about the poet. I stop speaking.

Agata asks, Then what?

Well, later he became an alcoholic, which saved his life when again he wanted to kill himself, this time with a large stone and a rope in the sea between the Korean Peninsula and Jeju Island.

Where is that? asks Autje, but she is shushed by her mother.

It doesn't matter, says Mejal.

Well, says Salome, it matters, but let August finish his story first.

Agata nods at me to continue.

On the boat, I say, they sold alcoholic drinks. Ko Un thought: Why not have one before dying? He had one drink, then a second and a third . . . he got drunk and fell asleep. When he woke up, he was at the pier. He had missed his opportunity to kill himself, and the others were waiting for him because they had heard that the legendary monk and poet Ko Un was coming to their island. They hoped that he would stay there. So he did. And he was very happy there for some years.

After a pause, Mejal asks me if I'm finished and I tell her that I am.

The women do not speak but shuffle on their pails, clearing their throats. I mutter that Agata had asked me if I had an opinion on the debate over leaving versus fleeing. I had meant only to articulate my feelings about the meaning of meaning: How it is possible to leave something or someone in one frame of mind and arrive elsewhere, in another entirely unexpected frame of mind.

I am already aware of that, says Mejal. Aren't we all?

We are aware of many things, instinctively, says Ona quietly, but to have them articulated in a certain narrative way is pleasing and fun.

Salome Friesen tells the women she has no time for pleasing and fun. May I be excused, she asks sarcastically, since it is lunchtime and my turn to bring food to a few of the elders of the colony as well as administer my youngest daughter's antibiotics?

Salome's youngest daughter, Miep, was violated by the men on two or possibly three different occasions, but Peters denied medical treatment for Miep, who is three years of age, on the grounds that the doctor would gossip about the colony and that people would become aware of the attacks and the whole incident would be blown out of proportion. Salome walked twelve miles to the next colony to procure antibiotics for Miep from the Mobile Klinic that she knew was stationed there, temporarily, for repairs. (And to pick up moonshine for herself, according to Mariche, who on several occasions when Salome is raging has indicated, by miming the act of bringing a bottle to her mouth, that Salome secretly drinks.)

I have to hide the antibiotics in Miep's strained beets or she won't swallow them, says Salome.

The women nod and tell her to go, go.

As she leaves, Salome suggests that if Mejal goes to get the soup from the summer kitchen then Salome could bring the spelt bread she baked this morning. We will all have this food for lunch, Salome says, and continue with our meeting as we eat. We will have instant coffee.

Mejal shrugs, languidly—she hates to be told what to do by Salome—but rises from her chair.

Agata, meanwhile, remains perfectly still, mouthing the words to a prayer or a verse, perhaps one from Psalms. Miep is her granddaughter, named after her. ("Miep" is a nickname.) Agata is a strong woman but whenever she hears the specific details of the attack on her tiny granddaughter she becomes very still, predatory.

(When Salome discovered that Miep had been attacked not once but two or three times, she went to the shed where the men were being kept and attempted to kill them all with a scythe, as I mentioned earlier. This was the incident that convinced Peters to call the police and have the men arrested and brought to the city where they would be safe. Salome claims she did ask to be forgiven for that outburst, and that the men forgave her, but nobody, including Peters, witnessed this. Perhaps these last facts are not germane to the minutes of the meetings but I believe they're significant enough to include in the footnotes because without the perpetrators having been taken to the city, and the other men of the colony following them to post bail in order to have them returned to the colony, where they could be forgiven by the victims and in turn have the victims forgiven by God, these meetings would not be happening.)

The Lord is gracious and compassionate, slow to anger, rich in loving kindness and forgiving, says Agata.

She repeats this, and Greta takes Agata's hand and joins her in the recitation.

Mejal Loewen has left the room, I presume to smoke, even though she has declared that she is going to get the soup from the summer kitchen. She ordered Autje, her niece, not to follow her, and Autje made a face as if to say, Why would I bother? And also a face to the others, as if to apologize for her strange aunt, the smoker with the secret life.

Miep and the other little children from the colony are being looked after by several young women at the home of Nettie Gerbrandt, whose husband is away in the city with the others. Nettie Gerbrandt's twin brother, Johan, is one of the eight on trial. Miep herself is unaware of why she experiences pain in certain parts of her small body, or that she has a sexually transmitted illness. Nettie Gerbrandt, too, was attacked, possibly by her brother, and gave birth prematurely to a baby boy so tiny he fit into her shoe. He died hours after being born and Nettie smeared her bedroom walls with blood. She has stopped talking, except to the children of the colony, which is why she has been put in charge of their care while the others work.

Mariche Loewen believes that Nettie may have changed her name to Melvin. She believes Nettie has done this because she no longer wants to be a woman. Agata and Greta refuse to believe this.

I ask for a quick breather.

Ona Friesen once again glances at me inquisitively—or perhaps she is curious at the notion of a "breather" (which, likely, is not a word she has ever heard before, even in translation), or at the notion of the sustained breath, the exquisite agony of the unexpressed thought, the narrative of life, the thread that binds, that knots, that holds. A breather, breath, sustained. The narrative.

The women give me their consent.

I have returned to the meeting. I am alone, waiting for the women.

When I was out, I heard music coming from a truck. It was the song "California Dreamin'," sung by the Mamas and the Papas on a radio turned to an oldies station. I stood a hundred metres from the truck, which was on the main road that runs along the perimeter of the colony. Autje and Neitje were standing beside it, listening. There were few sounds other than the voices of the Mamas and the Papas, in such sweet harmony, singing about the safety and warmth of Los Angeles, the dream of it. The girls didn't see me, I'm quite sure. They stood perfectly still beside the driver's side of the truck, their necks bent, heads down, as though they were forensic detectives listening for clues, or solemn mourners at a gravesite.

Before the song had played, the driver of the truck made a public announcement on his loudspeaker, which he had attached to the cab. He was an official census-taker and he insisted that all colonists must come out of their homes to be counted. He made this announcement several times but of course there are only women, mostly, now in the colony and they don't understand his language, and even if they did, they would not leave their homes, the barn, the summer kitchen, the yearling pen, the chicken coops, the laundry building . . . to be accounted for by a man driving a truck with a radio tuned to a pop station. Except for Autje and Neitje, of course, who were drawn to the truck like lost sailors to sirens.

Now, as I wait for the women to return to the meeting, I have the song "California Dreamin'" in my head, an earworm. I imagine teaching the women the lyrics to the song, having them harmonize like the Mamas and the Papas, repeating the lyrics, a call and response. I think they would enjoy it. *All the leaves are brown* . . . I gaze around the empty space, hearing their voices.

These meetings are taking place in the hayloft belonging to Earnest Thiessen, one of the elderly and infirm men who has not travelled to the city. Earnest is oblivious to most things, including the fact that the women are using his hayloft for their meetings. He can't remember how many children he's had or if his siblings are alive or dead, but one thing he has never forgotten is that Peters stole his clock. Earnest's father had left Earnest the family's cherished clock when he died, knowing that Earnest, of all of his sons and daughters, was most bound by and fascinated by the nature of time. Peters insisted that Earnest hand over the clock, telling him that time in Molotschna was eternal, that life on earth naturally flowed into life in heaven if one was pure in God's eyes, and therefore that time, and clocks, was irrelevant. It was discovered, months later, that Peters had installed the clock in his study, the room in his house where he planned his sermons and conducted colony business. Earnest, although senile, has never forgotten his stolen clock, as though this one injustice has expanded to take up all of his mind, as though he has been appointed as the keeper of this one injustice to the exclusion of all else, and when he sees Peters he always asks him when, at what time, will he return the clock.

The women prefer to meet in this hayloft rather than at one of their kitchen tables because in the kitchens there are children everywhere and always underfoot. It's not unusual for a family to have fifteen children. Or twenty-five children. (A few months ago, I gave myself a challenge: that I would walk down the main path that encircles Molotschna, through the cornfields and the sorghum, a distance of several miles, and only take a breath when I saw a child. My breathing never once faltered.)

Our table consists of hay bales with a piece of plywood laid across them, and our chairs are milking buckets. Autje and Neitje occasionally take turns sitting on the window ledge with their legs up and bent at the knees, or in saddles that they've removed from Earnest Thiessen's tack room and set up on a mouldy beam here in the loft.

Ona Friesen keeps an empty feed pail beside her because she is pregnant and is experiencing nausea. Several of the women in the colony attempted, hurriedly, when it was clear that Ona was expecting, to marry Ona to Julius Penner, the simple son of Ondrej Penner. But Ona insisted that Julius deserved better than a woman afflicted with Narfa and that he would be tainted with sin for marrying a woman who was not a virgin. The elders of the colony have concluded that Ona is beyond redemption, that her Narfa has rendered her incapable of reasoning. I feel obliged to point out that this criticism (being incapable of reasoning) from the elders is *saturated* in irony, and that Ona will be exempt from eternal damnation because she has not willfully sinned. Her unborn child, a product of the unwelcome visitors, as the rapists are euphemistically referred to by the elders, will be given to another colony family to raise as their own, perhaps even to the family of the unwelcome visitor.

Now the women are returning, with the exception of Autje and Neitje.

Mariche Loewen explains that the young women are at the end of Earnest Thiessen's driveway visiting with the Koop brothers from Chortiza, the neighbouring colony. (I know that isn't quite true, but suspect Mariche understands the blowback the girls would receive from Salome if Salome were to learn that they had been listening to the census-taker's radio. Mariche is protecting them, and saving time. Salome is such a puzzling contradiction,

defiant yet traditional, combative and rebellious yet eager
to enforce the rules when it comes to others.)

The other women frown, but concur that we must
begin without them.

Salome asks Mejal if she was smoking, and Mejal asks
Salome if that is any of her business. The two of them
have brought the bread and soup, and instant coffee, from
the summer kitchen and are serving portions of it for the
women, and for me.

Greta and Agata begin the meeting by stating that it
is imperative that we make a decision this afternoon about
staying or leaving.

But as they finish speaking, Autje and Neitje return
to the hayloft, and now they are entertaining us with an
amusing stunt. Before joining us in the loft they secretly
positioned a flatbed wagon carrying stacks of bales
underneath the window. Autje climbs the ladder first,
moaning hysterically about not being able to live a second longer, about life being too cruel. She sways and
moans, then runs to the window and flings herself out of
it, headfirst.

The women scream, and we all sprint and hobble to
the window, to find Autje sitting placidly atop the stack of
bales. Ona laughs hard in appreciation while the others
shake their heads and strive to contain any sign of approval.

The women resume their seats at the table. Neitje mentions that the Koop brothers told her and Autje—(now I
realize that the young women *did* visit with the Koop boys,
in addition to the census-taker)—that the brothers' father
had been in the city selling cheese and had bumped into

Ingersoll (Mariche's brother-in-law and husband of one of the Do Nothing women). Ingersoll was in the city with the other men from Molotschna and had stepped outside the courtroom to check on his team. He had told their father, who had mentioned it to their other brother, who then mentioned it to the Koop boys, that two of the Molotschna men were planning to return early to get extra livestock, and possibly horses, to auction in the city for more bail money.

Greta has lifted her arms into the air.

Agata sharpens her gaze (I see now that Salome has inherited this type of heat-seeking-missile gaze from her mother) and is very still.

How early? Mariche asks, and the young women shrug.

Which men? Mariche asks.

One of them is Klaas, says Neitje. (Klaas Loewen is Mariche's husband.)

Mariche takes a slender chicken bone from her mouth and lays it next to her bowl, and makes the smallest of small sounds.

Ona hands me a large roll of brown paper, the kind used to package cheese and meat. She tells me she has taken it from the summer kitchen.

My mother, Monica, used to give me cheese packaging paper to draw on when I was young.

Ona suggests that I use the packaging paper to make lists of the pros and cons for the women's options. These need to be written on a large piece of paper. None of the women will be able to read what you write, says Ona, but we will keep it here in the hayloft as an artifact for others to discover.

Autje and Neitje exchange glances. What is Ona talking about now? Why is she so strange? How can we prevent ourselves from becoming like her?

Yes, a discovery, says Salome (in a rare tender moment of indulging her sister).

Agata nods impatiently and moves her hands in rapid circles like a buggy wheel, meaning: Can we please proceed?

Mejal finds nails in the tack room (she will use any opportunity to indulge in a quick haul from her cigarette) and a salt block to hammer the packaging paper to the wall.

Ona suggests I write the first heading to read as follows: *Staying and Fighting*. Beneath that, I write a second sub-heading: *Pros*.

At this, the women begin speaking over one another, and I have no choice but to politely, and with apologies, request that they take turns speaking so that I can understand what each one of them is saying and have several seconds to transcribe it onto the paper.

PROS

We won't have to leave.

We won't have to pack.

We won't have to figure out where we're going or experience the uncertainty of not knowing where we are going. (We don't have a map of any place.)

Salome scoffs at this last point, calling it absurd. The only certainty we'll know is uncertainty, she says, regardless of where we are.

Ona asserts: Other than the certainty of the power of love.

Salome turns to face Ona directly. Keep inanities such as these to yourself, she pleads.

Mejal defends Ona. Why couldn't that be the case, that the only certainty is the power of love? she wonders.

Because it's meaningless! Salome shouts. Particularly in this fucking context!

Agata sharply rebukes her daughters. Then, deflecting, she points to the younger women. Autje? Neitje? she says. Do you have something to add to the list?

Salome is tearing off slivers of her fingernails with her teeth and eating them. Mejal grimaces in disgust as Salome spits out the nails.

We won't have to leave the people we love? says Neitje.

Greta points out that the women could bring loved ones with them.

Others question the practicality of this, and Ona mentions, gently, that several of the people we love are people we also fear.

We could create the possibility of a new order right here, in a place that is familiar to us, Mariche adds.

Not simply familiar, a place that *is* ours, corrects Salome.

But if we leave it, asks Mejal, will it still be ours? Will we be able to come back?

August did, says Salome. Ask him.

There's no time, says Ona. August, write the cons now please.

I embrace Ona, in my mind, and she embraces me.

CONS

We won't be forgiven.

We don't know how to fight. (Salome interrupts: I know how to fight. The others studiously ignore her.)

We don't want to fight.

There is the risk that conditions will be worse after fighting than before.

Ona raises her hand and asks if she may speak. (I wonder if she is doing this sarcastically, in response to my earlier comment to the women about speaking in turn.)

Please, I say to her.

Would it be beneficial, Ona asks, before we list the pros and cons of staying and fighting, to establish what exactly we are fighting for?

Mariche quickly responds: It's obvious: we're fighting for our safety and for our freedom from attacks!

Yes, Ona agrees, but what would that entail? Perhaps we need to create a manifesto or revolutionary statement— (Ona and I glance quickly at each other; I know that she is invoking my mother, who was forever, in fields and barns and by candlelight, working on versions of revolutionary statements. I look down and smile)—that describes the conditions of life in the colony that we would aspire to/ require after winning the fight. Perhaps we need to know more specifically what we are fighting to achieve (not only what we are fighting to destroy), and what actions would be required for such achievement, even after the fight has been won, if it is won.

When Ona speaks, says Mariche, it sounds like a stampede of yearlings in my head. There is not enough time left for this kind of discussion. She reminds the women that a certain number of the men are returning early to the colony.

Agata agrees with Mariche, placating her. But she also reminds the women that their meetings and plans could be kept secret from the two or three men returning early, and that these men will only be at the colony briefly to pick up more animals to sell, and will quickly return to the city. Since Mariche's husband, Klaas, is rumoured to be one of the men returning early, Agata reminds Mariche that she must "act natural," as it were. (Agata has used a Low German expression for which there is no easy translation to English. It pertains to a type of fruit and to winter.)

The others nod in solemn agreement.

Agata continues, asking Ona to elaborate on her revolutionary statement.

I notice that even Neitje and Autje, who are normally wary of Ona because Ona is thought to have lost her fear— which is akin, for colonists, to having lost one's moral compass and been transformed into a demon—have turned their attention to her.

It's very simple, says Ona.

She tosses off a few ideas: Men and women will make all decisions for the colony collectively. Women will be allowed to think. Girls will be taught to read and write. The schoolhouse must display a map of the world so that we can begin to understand our place in it. A new religion, extrapolated from the old but focused on love, will be created by the women of Molotschna.

(I feel pain in my chest. Ona is repeating nearly verbatim one of the lessons my mother, Monica, gave to the girls in her secret schoolhouse. She is looking at me, trying to make eye contact, she is attempting to communicate something vital, something remembered, something lost.)

Mariche creases her brow, dramatically.

Ona continues: Our children will be safe.

Greta has closed her eyes. She repeats the word "collectively," as though it is the name of a new vegetable she is unfamiliar with.

Mariche can contain herself no longer. She accuses Ona of being a dreamer.

We are women without a voice, Ona states calmly. We are women out of time and place, without even the language of the country we reside in. We are Mennonites without a homeland. We have nothing to return to, and even the animals of Molotschna are safer in their homes than we women are. All we women have are our dreams— so of course we are dreamers.

Mariche scoffs at this. Would you like to hear *my* dream? she asks, and before anyone can reply she begins to describe a dream in which people with Narfa are not put in charge of making revolutionary statements.

Ona is smiling—not nervously but with genuine appreciation for Mariche's humour.

Ona and Salome's younger sister Mina had a reputation in the colony as a perpetual smiler. She was Happy Mina. Ona is smiling like Mina now.

(Even in death, Mina appeared to be smiling. At Mina's funeral, Ona pulled Mina's kerchief down an inch or two to reveal the rope marks on her neck. She said in a loud voice to the congregation that it wasn't ammonia from cleaning the barn that had killed her, as Peters had said. Mina had been found hanging from a rafter in the yearling shed. Peters had interrupted Mina's funeral service and asked Deacons Klippenstein and Unrau to take Ona home. The funeral was being held outside the church because the bodies of suicides are not permitted in the sanctuary. Mina's body lay on a block of ice, in the sun. Mina sank lower and lower, towards the ground, slowly enclosed by a dark circle, wet earth. Ona ran away from the men. Peters prayed for Ona. The congregation bowed their heads.

Neitje is Mina's daughter, now in the care of Salome. Mina hanged herself after Neitje was attacked in her bedroom, her wrists rubbed raw with baler twine, her body smeared with blood and shit and semen. At first Peters told Mina it was Satan who was responsible for the attack, that it was punishment from God, that God was punishing the women for their sins. Then Peters told Mina she was making the attack up. He repeated the words "wild female imagination," with forceful punctuation after each of the words to create three short sentences. Mina demanded to know which it was: Satan or her imagination. Mina clawed at Peters' eyes. She removed her clothes and damaged her body with pinking shears. She went to the barn and hanged herself. Peters cut her down and told the colony she had inhaled too many ammonia fumes while cleaning the yearling shed. Agata Friesen, Mina's mother, washed Mina's body in her own tears. That is what the women of the colony say, and they were there.)

Agata now indicates that she's heard enough. She declares that the revolutionary statement Ona outlined earlier is sound, and can be added to in the course of time, and that it will stand as the manifesto boldly declaring what the women want to happen in the colony if they are to stay and fight.

Greta has raised both arms in the air. She asks: What will happen if the men refuse to meet our demands?

Ona responds: We will kill them.

Autje and Neitje gasp, then smile tentatively.

Mejal is so perturbed that she has taken out her rolling papers and tobacco in full view of the others.

Agata stands up and puts her arms around Ona. No *leibchen*, she whispers, no. She explains to the others that Ona is joking.

Salome shrugs. *Maybe not.*

Agata pokes Salome in the shoulder, and says: We will find a road and we will travel.

Greta nods slowly. Yes, but then what are you saying, Agata? That we will leave?

A road is many things, Agata tells her.

This type of "Friesen talk" (what Mariche characterizes as "coffeehousing," although she has never been to a coffee house) exasperates the Loewens.

Autje gingerly suggests that we now list the pros and cons for leaving, and the others agree.

Autje and Neitje, I notice, have removed their kerchiefs and braided their long hair together, into one braid, so they are conjoined.

LEAVING

PROS

We will be gone.

We will be safe.

Mariche interjects here. Perhaps not, she says, but the first is most definitely a fact, that if we leave we will be gone. She looks around at the group. Are we not under too much of a time restriction to state the obvious?

Salome snaps back that not everything is to be interpreted literally. She adds to the list.

> We will not be asked to forgive the men,
> because we will not be here to hear the
> question.

Yes, says Mariche, sarcastically—but according to Ona's manifesto, new methods of forgiveness would be established and the men would not be allowed to force us to forgive, or force us to leave the colony if we don't forgive, or threaten us with God's refusal to forgive us if we don't forgive the men. She reminds us that one of Ona's earlier notions was that harm done to children, because of its abjectly depraved nature, should be in its own God-only forgiveness category, and that Ona seems to think she has the authority to create a new religion.

Ona protests, quietly, that she doesn't believe that at all. She doesn't believe in authority, period, because authority makes people cruel.

Salome interrupts: The people with authority or the people without?

Mariche ignores Salome. How on earth can you not believe in authority? she asks Ona.

How on earth *can* you believe in authority? says Ona.

Greta and Agata, in unison, beg both women to be silent.

We will see a little bit of the world? This "pro" is offered by Neitje Friesen.

I observe that as the older women's patience begins to unravel, the younger women are stepping with trepidation into the breach. They are still connected to each other with their hair. Once again, the lyrics of "California Dreamin'" come to mind and I hum, *All the leaves are brown* . . .

A few of the women look at me, curious—especially Autje and Neitje. Perhaps they are wondering why I'm humming the song they heard on the census-taker's radio. Had I been spying on them? I'd like to explain to them that I wasn't spying, it was an accident, but I know I cannot.

I request that we move on to the Cons of Leaving.

Mariche reminds me that they, the women, will determine what happens in these meetings, not a "two-bit" failed farmer, a *schinda* who must resort to teaching.

Greta erupts. Mariche! she shouts, standing up. Klaas is returning any minute and you are wasting time with your irritability! Klaas will return to your home for just long enough to take his animals in order to sell for bail money that will see the rapists return to Molotschna, and he will lay his hands on you and on the children, and you, as always, will say nothing to him but rather fire away at us all like a Gatling gun with your misdirected rage. What good does that do?

The women are silent.

I apologize for wrongly attempting to nudge the proceedings, as that is not my place.

The women say nothing. Greta is heaving with each breath.

Note: The word Mariche used to describe me, *schinda*, means "tanner," a tanner of hides. In Russia, when Mennonites lived by the Black Sea with its mysterious underground river, men who were unable to make a living as farmers were forced to herd the cattle for the other Mennonites. If a cow died, the herdsman had to skin the animal and tan the hide. *Schinda*, therefore, means one not clever enough to know how to farm. It is the king of insults in Molotschna.

Now Greta speaks, and she makes a radical statement. She says that she is no longer a Mennonite.

Autje and Neitje, experts though they are at appearing indifferent, look up from the table, alarmed.

Ona mentioned earlier that we women would have to ask ourselves who we were, Greta says. Well, she declares, I have told you who I am not.

Agata is laughing. She claims that Greta has many times announced that she is no longer a Mennonite—and yet was born from Mennonites and continues to live as a Mennonite, with Mennonites, in a Mennonite colony, where she speaks the Mennonite language.

Those things do not make me a Mennonite, Greta argues.

Then what are the things that make you a Mennonite? Agata asks.

Autje, in what I think must be an attempt to restore order, has piped up again, suggesting several Cons to Leaving.

We don't have a map, she says.

But the other women ignore her, listening to Agata and Greta's debate.

Autje and Neitje sway back and forth, a tug of war with the braid that connects them, but gently. Autje continues: We don't know where to go.

Neitje laughs. She adds: We don't even know where we are!

The girls laugh together.

At last Greta turns to them, hollering, Hush! And: Put your hair away.

Miep, Salome's little daughter, has climbed up the ladder to the loft and is calling out to her mother. Salome picks Miep up into her arms. Miep is crying. She is frightened. She has heard the women yelling. Miep asks Salome to change her diaper—but shyly, because she is three years old already.

Agata explains to me softly that Miep had been out of diapers for nearly a year but had recently requested to wear them again.

Salome is holding Miep and stroking her hair, whispering to her, kissing her. Ona puts her arm around Salome's shoulders while her sister cradles Miep.

Should we adjourn for the day? Agata suggests.

Mejal nods but asks that at least one or two of the Cons of Leaving be written on the packaging paper so that the women and I will know where to start tomorrow—or later this evening, if it is possible to leave their homes.

Salome stands up, holding Miep.

None, she says. There are no Cons of Leaving.

I imagine her leaving this very moment, becoming smaller and smaller as, with Miep in her arms, she walks across the soybean field, the coffee field, the cornfield, the sorghum, the crossing, the dry riverbed, the coulee, across the border, never once turning around for a last salty look.

And the gates of hell shall not prevail against her.

Please sit, says Agata, touching Salome's arm.

Salome obeys her mother. She sits, and glares into the middle distance.

Now Nettie (Melvin) Gerbrandt has climbed the ladder to the loft and is presenting herself to the women. She apologizes for letting Miep out of her sight, for allowing Miep to run away to her mother, although she says all this without using words.

Agata waves the apology away. Not to worry, she says kindly, and encourages Nettie to return to the other children, who have likely been left alone. Miep will stay with Salome for now.

Nettie nods vigorously and climbs back down the ladder.

We all know Nettie is exhausted, Agata remarks to the others.

(Nettie doesn't talk, except to the children, but at night the members of the colony can hear her screaming in her sleep—or perhaps screaming in full consciousness.)

Agata suggests that the women sing to Miep, and Greta agrees.

The teenagers, Autje and Neitje, are once again visibly distressed by this request, although they do join the other women in a melodic rendition of "Children of the Heavenly Father."

Ona smiles at me. (Or perhaps she smiled at no one in particular and only I have noticed it.)

In song (and perhaps in song alone) the women's voices soar in perfect harmony. Miep snuggles against her mother's breast.

I should include the lyrics here but the truth is I've forgotten most of them (crowded out by "California Dreamin'") and can't write quickly enough. I'll worship silently while the women sing for little Miep. I'm remembering my father. I'm remembering my mother. I'm remembering life, the scent of my mother's hair, the warmth of my father's back beneath the sun, bent towards the earth, his laughter, my mother running towards me, my faith. Without a homeland to return to, we return to our faith. Faith is our homeland. Great is Thy faithfulness, the song in my head, my mind, my thoughts, my intellect, my home, my funeral—but not my death.

The day is coming to an end. The singing has ended. The cows are demanding to be milked. The flies have left their shady hide-outs and are flinging themselves at filthy glass. Dueck's dogs are barking for their dinner, but Dueck is in the city and he is the only one who would care to feed them.

As if my thoughts can be heard, Mariche says that she'll throw some meat at Dueck's dogs later this evening to prevent them from attacking any of the children.

The distinctive odours of dill and roasted sausage have managed to travel all the way from the summer kitchen to Earnest Thiessen's hayloft.

Greta asks for consensus: Can we agree that tomorrow morning, she says, we will arrive at a decision about whether to stay or to leave, and then implement that decision?

Each woman, in turn, and in her individual fashion, agrees. But when it is her turn, Mejal Loewen raises a point. If the women do leave the colony, she asks, how will we live with the anguish of not seeing our loved ones again, our husbands and our brothers, the men?

It appears that Salome is about to speak, but Mejal raises her hand, stops her.

Salome whispers to Mejal. Miep stirs in her arms, but is quiet. Mejal smiles.

The two women laugh, briefly, and whisper again. Which man? asks Salome.

Stop, says Mejal. (Does she have a secret life?)

Mariche, it seems, is eager to end the meeting. The menfolk can accompany the women, she says, if they choose to, but only if they sign and adhere to the conditions of the manifesto.

Ona asks Mariche, politely, if she hadn't earlier dismissed the manifesto as a toothless document?

Mariche opens her mouth, but Salome quickly interjects. Time will heal our heavy hearts, she states. Our freedom and safety are the ultimate goals, and it is men who prevent us from achieving those goals.

But not all men, says Mejal.

Ona clarifies: Perhaps not men, per se, but a pernicious ideology that has been allowed to take hold of men's hearts and minds.

Neitje, alarmed now that the implications are sinking in, asks if it is true that if the women choose to leave, she will never see her brothers again?

(I should explain here that in the colony there is a loose commitment to the conventional definition of brothers and sisters. Men and women, boys and girls, address each other as brother and sister—and in fact, every colony member is related, closely.)

Autje asks: Who will take care of our brothers?

Agata Friesen, her expression one of concern, requests that the women resume their seats. These are important questions, she says solemnly. And we must resolve them before we make our final decision to stay or to leave.

Fair enough, says Greta. Strands of white hair have escaped her kerchief and she is blowing on the wisps from the side of her mouth. Her teeth remain on the plywood table. She asks: But what of the milking and supper preparations?

This is met with blank stares from the women in the hayloft.

I laugh, for some reason I don't fully understand, then quickly apologize. I see that Miep has fallen asleep in Salome's arms.

Agata asks, in what appears to be a supreme act of mercy towards the younger ladies, if the others in attendance would permit Autje and Neitje to leave the meeting in order to assist the colony women with the evening chores.

But Salome objects. It is the younger ladies, Autje and Neitje, she points out, who have posed certain pertinent questions regarding boys and men. They should be expected to remain in the meeting in order to participate in the discussion pertaining to those questions and, most importantly, to be privy to the answers we attach to those questions.

Keep them here, then, for the love of Joshua Judges Ruth! shouts Mariche.

Agata smiles, twists her body from side to side (a thing she does when she is pleased or delighted). I like that expression, she says.

Salome, feigning shock, says, I didn't know, Mariche, that you were so familiar with the chronology of the books of the Bible, as you never seem to be in possession of that Good Book.

Greta rests her hand on Mariche's arm—to warn her not to respond to Salome's comment. She whispers something, perhaps acknowledging Mariche's fear that Klaas will be home soon and there is no dinner ready.

Autje and Neitje, caught in this crossfire among their elders, are statues.

Agata takes a deep breath. She addresses the unspoken fears of the women. The milking and supper preparations will easily be taken care of by the women "on the ground," she says. And the women's future is better served by us remaining in the hayloft for now and hammering out these last-minute concerns.

Ona says: I wouldn't necessarily categorize the future of our relationships with the boys and men we love as "last-minute concerns."

She may have glanced in my direction when she said this, but I cannot tell for certain. "My" direction is in the same direction as the window (directly behind me), which is filthy and crawling with flies and looks out at the miles and miles of fields and sky and galaxies beyond that, and then infinity. So perhaps not.

The women settle in for more discussion. Shadows fall on their faces and upon the piece of plywood set up to be their table. I have spotted several mice—or is it the same mouse, an exceptionally active one? Autje and Neitje, still comically conjoined, are using their kerchiefs to swipe at flies.

(Technically these kerchiefs are to be worn by all women over the age of fifteen in the presence of men. I have never seen Autje's and Neitje's hair before. It looks very soft—blonde in the case of Neitje, with varying shades from nearly white to golden to beige, and in the case of Autje, dark brown with a discreet auburn glaze, a colour that matches her eyes and also the manes and tails of Ruth and Cheryl, Greta's skittish team. I am ashamed to admit that I wonder if Autje and Neitje do not consider me enough of a man, or really one at all, to warrant covering their hair in my presence.)

Agata is barefoot now. She raises her legs and props them on a piece of wood to reduce the fluid build-up she suffers from. Edema, she calls it. There is a note of pride in her voice when she says the word "edema." (There must be satisfaction gained in accurately naming the thing that torments you.)

Salome has laid Miep down on a saddle blanket beside her, and the child is the focal point of the assembled women.

Agata has asked me to print in large letters:

OPTIONS FOR THE MEN AND
OLDER BOYS IF THE WOMEN
DECIDE TO LEAVE:

1. That they be allowed to leave with the
   women if they wish.

2. That they be allowed to leave with the
   women only if they sign the declaration/
   manifesto.

3. That they be left behind.

4. That they be allowed to join the women
   later, when the women have determined
   where they're going and have established
   themselves and are thriving as a demo-
   cratic/collective/literate community
   (with progress reports made regularly
   on the rehabilitation/behaviour of the
   men and boys with regard to the women
   and girls).

   NB. Boys under the age of twelve, simple-
   minded boys of any age, Cornelius (a
   colony boy of fifteen who is confined
   to a wheelchair) and the elderly/infirm
   men who are unable to care for themselves (these are the boys and men
   who have remained here instead of
   going to the city) will automatically
   accompany the women.

For the first time since the commencement of the
meeting, the women appear to be genuinely perplexed.
They are silent, deep in thought.

Mariche speaks first. She votes for the first option.

This sits well with no one else. Voices are raised in unison and Mariche crosses her arms. She is anxious to leave. She tosses the dregs of her instant coffee onto the floor, says she'd like to strangle herself.

But Mariche, says Ona, the possibility arises of the men, perhaps all of them, choosing to leave with us, and all we'd be doing is re-creating our existing colony, with all of its inherent dangers, elsewhere, wherever we end up.

Agata adds: And the men would most definitely leave with us because they can't survive without us.

Greta laughs and says, Well, not for longer than a day or two.

Salome points out that option number one is really rather moot. If we do decide ultimately to leave the colony rather than to stay and fight, she says, we will leave the colony before the men return, so there is no possibility of the men leaving *with* us.

Mejal, now openly smoking (although, because it vexes Salome, making grand gestures of batting the smoke away from sleeping Miep), states that option number one is ridiculous and should be scratched off the list. She further states that option number two (allowing the men to leave with the women if the men sign the manifesto of demands) is, for the same reason as number one, moot. Furthermore, says Mejal, even if we did decide to leave only after the men have returned, and to take with us those of the men who agree to sign the manifesto, how do we know that their acts of signing are not treacherous? Who, other than the women of Molotschna, could be more aware of the duplicity of men?

Well spoken, says Ona.

Mariche states: Well then, let's be done with it and leave the men behind. Number three it is! She slams the table (plywood) with her fist, and Miep stirs.

Salome asks Mariche to restrain herself.

You are going from one extreme to the other, Greta protests to Mariche. First allowing any men to leave with us if they want to, and now leaving them all behind.

Then why, Mariche asks, if option numbers one and three are extreme, moot or preposterous, were they allowed to be written down in the first place? To waste time? To provide August Epp more time to practise his letters?

August Epp doesn't need any more practice, Ona murmurs. Perhaps Mariche is envious of his ability to write.

Mariche assures Ona that she is not envious of an effeminate man who is unable to properly till a field or eviscerate a hog.

Order! Agata insists. Clearly option numbers one and three, as evident in the minutes, are unrealistic and untenable. Option number two is suspect, in that we women cannot be confident that the presence of the men's signatures on our manifesto wouldn't be meaningless, or that they would have been made in good faith.

So, says Greta, it would appear that our only remaining option is option number four.

(As a reminder: This is the option that allows the men to join the women later, subject to certain conditions.)

Mariche says, Well, you mean the only remaining option that has been written down on the packaging paper.

Yes, agrees Agata. But these are the options we have mutually arrived at and we do require a system of some kind. If there are other options, they cannot reside within our minds only—we need to state them and have them documented.

According to you, says Mariche. I carry many options around with me in my head.

But, says Greta, those don't help us now, do they? We don't know what they are and if they're viable. Would you like to tell us what they are, if they are significantly different from the options we have already collectively agreed on, and which August Epp has so kindly inscribed on paper?

Mariche is silent.

Autje says: I like number four.

Neitje says: Me too.

Agata smiles at the young women. Both Autje and Neitje have younger and older brothers, along with fathers and male cousins, that they wish to see again one day.

Would everyone consent to option number four, asks Greta, with the proviso that our minds might be changed in the future? And that any change must be undertaken with one goal in mind: the safety of the girls and women, and the likeliness of rehabilitation of the men and boys, of Molotschna?

Oh! Salome's rage has turned to tears, a stunning development. She presses her index fingers into the corners of her eyes, near the bridge of her nose, pushing back the tears.

(I am reminded of how Ona ends her sentences with a sharp intake of breath, inhaling her words back into herself, safe. If the women implement option number four, Salome's beloved son Aaron will be left behind with the men because he is over twelve years of age. Though just barely.

Aaron is a good-natured boy with an easy grace, and one of my exceptional students, although he will be leaving school soon for good to help the older men in the fields. Aaron holds the colony title for fence walking. With his innate ability to balance, he is able to walk on the three-inch-wide top beam, the entire length of the fence that encloses the paddock belonging to the yearling barn. The boys and I fashioned a trophy for him out of various bits of machinery, wood and twine, and Cornelius, our resident pyrographer, expertly inscribed Aaron's name and title into the bottom part of the trophy, in cursive! The trophy was confiscated from Aaron by Peters who warned him—and the next day, all of us—of the consequences—vague, though including flesh-eating worms—of vanity and pride.

On that morning, the morning that Peters confiscated Aaron's trophy, I excused myself from the classroom and walked into the field behind the school. I stood and prayed. I knelt and prayed. I listened for God's words, an answer. But all I could hear were my own thoughts, coiled snakes, and the venom of my words, which were: *Today I have come to understand arson.* I imagined my students, the young boys of Molotschna, alone in the classroom waiting for me—or not waiting for me, making mischief, throwing animal turds, laughing, sneering, cowering, begging, snapping suspenders, snatching hats, the littlest ones with frozen smiles praying for me to return, to silence the big boys, to restore order, me, the teacher, who, with only one desire, to burn it all down, to burn it to the ground, was on his knees, weeping, in the field behind the classroom.

In jail, one of my cellmates who misheard that I was an arsonist, not an anarchist or an Antichrist, spoke to me about his feelings, a complex web of fire, anger and destruction. I pretended to listen closely because I was afraid of him. Would he have spoken to me about his feelings if he had known the truth?)

Agata has put her arm around Salome's shoulders. She says to Salome that the sadness of leaving Aaron behind for the time being will only spur her, Salome, and the other grieving mothers, to rebuild a new and better colony for everyone.

Mejal is upset now, too, although she doesn't have a son to leave behind. She and Salome spend a great deal of time at odds, but always come together as a united force during crises. Now Mejal crosses to Salome's side of the plywood in order to embrace her fully.

But why, asks Salome, if fifteen-year-old boys are already in the city with the men (fifteen is the age of baptism and full-fledged membership in the church), and boys twelve and under are allowed to join the women, are boys aged thirteen and fourteen left to the dubious care and instruction of the men? Why are the boys in this slender category not also allowed to accompany us if we leave? And what if the rapists are released on bail and return to the colony and find that there are no girls and women here, and begin to use these boys, the thirteen- and fourteen-year-olds, as targets for their attacks?

Mejal chimes in: Surely we can't be afraid of boys this age? Why couldn't they join us?

Ona now startles me with a question. August, she says, you're the boys' teacher. What is your feeling about this? Do boys of this age pose a threat to our girls and women?

I must stop my transcribing in order to properly answer her question. I'm simply not capable of containing my happiness and surprise at being asked a question by Ona, formulating my answer, communicating it in Low German, and translating it instantly in my mind to English—while almost simultaneously writing the English translation down on paper. I will put my pen down momentarily while I attempt to answer Ona's question.

I have now picked up my pen again and the women are speaking amongst themselves.

(Ona has thanked me for a thoughtful response to the question. My joy is overwhelming and I'm struggling to suppress it. I wish I were able to turn myself to stone as easily as Neitje and Autje do. I feel that so many problems in my life may have been prevented if I'd been more . . . contained.)

My answer to Ona's question—do boys of thirteen and fourteen pose a threat to the girls and women of Molotschna Colony?—was yes, possibly. Every one of us, male or female, poses a potential threat. Thirteen- and fourteen-year-old boys are capable of causing great damage to girls and women, and to each other. It is a brash age. These boys are possessed of reckless urges, physical exuberance, intense curiosity that often results in injury, unbridled emotion, including deep tenderness and empathy, and not quite enough experience or brain development to fully understand or appreciate the consequences of their actions or words. They are similar to the yearlings: young, awkward, gleeful, powerful. They are tall, muscular, sexually inquisitive creatures with little impulse control, but they are children. They are children and they can be taught. I'm a two-bit schoolteacher, a failed farmer, a *schinda*, an effeminate man, and, above all, a believer. I believe that with direction, firm love and patience these boys, aged thirteen and fourteen, are capable of relearning their roles as males in the Molotschna Colony. I believe in what the great poet Samuel Taylor Coleridge thought were the cardinal rules of early education: "To work by love and so generate love. To habituate the mind to intellectual accuracy and truth. To excite imaginative power." In his Lecture on Education, Coleridge concluded with the words: "Little is taught by contest or dispute, everything by sympathy and love."

As I expressed this to the women, Ona had looked up, her eyes on me, and silently mouthed Coleridge's words with me. *Sympathy and love*. In her secret school, my mother had often quoted the words of Coleridge, her favourite of the Romantic poets, a metaphysical dreamer, in pain, mysterious, handsome.

I nodded to the women vigorously, on the verge of tears, a lunatic, a sad clown. I said: I believe those boys should be allowed to leave with the women, providing the women choose to leave.

Mariche is the first to respond. It was a "yes" or "no" question, she says. Why do you talk that way? You shit like any other man, why can't you talk like one?

I scratch my head. I am sorry, I tell her.

Ona ignores her. Instead, she asks me: August, what will you do here on the colony if there are no children to teach?

Before I can gather my wits to answer, Mariche says sarcastically, If nothing else surely it will be a good opportunity for August to learn the tools of a serious trade, like farming.

Perhaps the older boys could continue to attend classes, suggests Neitje. Those over fifteen, the ones who, as members of the church, will stay behind.

Autje nods. She (slyly) states: Several of them could benefit from remedial teaching.

Yes, says Neitje, fifteen-year-old boys still believe that throwing horse turds at the girls while we do the milking shows their love.

Autje laughs. But a boy who truly loves you will intentionally miss when he throws the shit, she says, or will not throw it with quite as much force.

Mejal and Salome shake their heads.

Salome states (her tears a thing of the past, successfully pushed back into her sockets and locked away) that her most fervent dream for little Miep is that one happy day a boy will intentionally miss hitting her with a clump of shit.

Yes, agrees Mejal, the day every mother dreams of, the hope that gets us through the darkest hours.

But those boys can't stay in school, objects Mariche. They are required to work the fields and tend to the animals. Their school is outside the classroom. And furthermore, she adds, if there are no women and girls here to help the men with the chores, those fifteen-year-old boys will be more needed than ever.

Assuming that farming will be the central occupation of the men left behind, says Ona.

What in the name of God's green earth else could it be? asks Mariche.

Ona shrugs. Surely there are other ways of being in the world.

But not for these men, objects Greta. They are certainly not scholars, not these men.

(I catch Autje and Neitje exchanging glances, mysteriously.)

Agata considers this point. Possibly, she says. But there are occupations other than scholar or farmer.

And then, in a moment I find serendipitous, because I had been reciting the same words to myself, silently, Ona quotes Virgil, from a poem my mother taught us in her secret schoolhouse. "Much service, too, does he who turns his plough, and again breaks crosswise through the ridges he raised."

I look up from my minutes and smile at Ona.

Is that from Leviticus? asks Mariche.

Yes, says Ona, correct, and I pretend to cough.

Mejal uses her finger and thumb to pinch out her cigarette, no doubt with the intention of saving it for later. Her fingertips are yellow—no, ochre.

So, says Mariche, the Bible endorses farming. That's clear. (She is glaring at me, I think, although one of her eyes is cloudy, veiled in white, from having a hoof pick flung at it, and it's not always clear where she's looking.)

But more than that, says Ona, it's a useful metaphor.

Agata, indulgent, acknowledges Ona's small fib with a nod but then pleads with her: My love, we're plotting to save our lives right now, so—

I'm aware of that, says Ona. I'm trying to help, and metaphors can be beneficial in this regard, and this particular line, this metaphor is so apt for the boys and men of Molotschna, for the—

Agata nods quickly. Yes, she agrees. She clamps her hand over Ona's, and again insists that the women move forward. She gazes deeply into Ona's eyes while she's saying this, begging. Agata's eyes are wet and bloodshot, pink and red veins streaking from a darker centre, setting suns.

Ona stops talking about metaphors.

Agata continues: We girls and women are considering leaving the colony, but has it been determined among us what we will do, how we will live, how we will support ourselves, when and if we leave? We're unable to read, we're unable to write, we're unable to speak the language of our country, we have only domestic skills that may or may not be required of us elsewhere in the world, and speaking of the world—we have no world map—

Mariche interrupts. Not this business with the world map again, she says.

I make a foray into the conversation, at the risk of

incurring Mariche's wrath, and suggest that I may be able to secure a world map for the women.

Ona asks: In short order?

I nod.

Mariche huffs, flares her nostrils.

Greta closes her eyes.

Agata straightens her back.

Neitje asks: From where?

I answer, From Chortiza.

The women are startled. In unison, they ask me how it is that the neighbouring Chortiza colony is in possession of such a map.

I'm unable to divulge that information, I explain, as a matter of safety—theirs—but it is quite likely that I could borrow the map for a short period of time, and that perhaps Autje and Neitje, with their artistic prowess, could copy it onto packaging paper.

The women, except Mariche, seem to find this proposition appealing.

Salome asks whether there might also be, in the Chortiza colony, a map of this specific region? It would be best, she wisely points out, if we were to have a very detailed map that included highways, minor roads, rivers and rail tracks, for instance. If such a map exists.

True, says Mariche. We aren't planning to traverse the planet.

Perhaps we are, counters Ona. She adds an interesting fact. Did you know, she says, that the migration period of butterflies and dragonflies is so long that it is often only the grandchildren who arrive at the intended destination?

As she speaks, Ona is beaming. She is again quoting, loosely, my mother. I want to thank Ona, I want to hug her. (No, what I really want is to pick her up and dance around the loft. When we were children, I scooped her up behind the yearling barn and ran a distance with her in my arms, laughing, as she told me not to crush her rib-cage or her heart would escape.)

Autje and Neitje smile back at Ona—although whether it is with genuine delight at the details of this dragonfly fact or simply because they have now been given an appropriate opportunity to smile and laugh broadly is unclear. I suspect they are laughing at the idiocy of their male peers while pretending to be greatly amused at the thought of little dragonfly grandchildren crossing an imaginary finish line having left the corpses of previous generations behind.

Mejal, meanwhile, nods her head at this curious fact.

Salome swats a fly away from Miep's open mouth. Miep's limbs have fallen loosely across the saddle blanket.

And did you know, says Ona, looking straight at me now and smiling broadly, that dragonflies have six legs but cannot walk?

I nod, yes. And also, I say, emboldened by Ona's glance, dragonflies have compound eyes that cover nearly their entire heads allowing them to see everything all at once, even the smallest, fastest movements.

Some of the women nod and ponder this. Autje and Neitje laugh.

So, I say, flustered. Yes, so.

I observe that Agata and Greta haven't heard the fact. Instead, they are talking in low voices between themselves, speculating on how a world map made it to Chortiza.

I whisper to Ona: There is a man, a musician named John Cage, who has composed a musical piece that will take over six hundred years to play. One note every few years, or even more. The notes are played on a special organ in a church in a small town in Germany.

Ona whispers back: Ah, so?

Me: Yes.

Ona: Is John Cage a Mennonite?

Me: No.

Ona: Ah.

Me: Well, perhaps he is.

Ona: Yes.

Now the women are enjoying a laugh together as they imagine what Peters would do if he found out that an illicit world map was being harboured just down the road from Molotschna.

Agata reminds us of the incident in which, on a particular Sunday, Peters held Earnest Thiessen's organic farming manuals up to the congregation as evidence of worldly influence. Earnest Thiessen was disciplined by the elders and forbidden contact with the colony members for a period of eight weeks. During those weeks he roamed about the country roads and slept in the tack room attached to the yearling barn. (Now that Earnest is senile—except for his everlasting memory of the stolen clock—which is a blessing, he has forgotten the evil of his former ways and is either fully convinced that God will welcome him, no holds barred, into His kingdom, or has no idea that God or God's kingdom even exist.)

Mariche attempts to bring us back to the discussion. She reminds me that Salome had asked a question.

Might there also be a regional map hiding out in Chortiza? Salome asks, repeating her question.

I venture to guess that it's possible.

Mariche asks if I will smuggle it out of Chortiza as well as the world map, and I promise that I will, if one exists. Mariche thanks me! And allows that I have a practical use after all. In her lexicon, a smuggler is preferable to a teacher, though not as esteemed as a farmer.

But August has had a practical use all along, says Ona. Who does Mariche think will explain the map to us if not August? Has Mariche, unbeknownst to the others, suddenly been blessed by God with an understanding of both geography and cartography?

Mariche swats away the question and tilts her head, points at the window with her bitten-off finger.

Ona makes a suggestion: Perhaps the women can create their own map as they go.

The others turn their attention to her, mystified.

Greta states: Now that is a unique idea—

She is interrupted by Ona, who has begun to vomit into the milk pail that sits beside her.

Greta says: Oh, *schatzi*.

Agata gets up—her legs have been elevated until now—and walks to Ona. She strokes her back and keeps the loose strands that Ona has allowed to escape from her kerchief from getting in the way of the projectile.

Ona lifts her head and reassures the women that she's fine.

The women nod. Their attention now turns to Mejal, who is breathing heavily. Her hand is on her chest.

Greta says, What now?

Are you okay, Mejal? asks Agata.

Mejal nods her head vigorously.

Salome explains quietly to me that Mejal is having one of her episodes. She goes to Mejal and whispers softly, inaudibly, in her ear. She holds Mejal's hand.

The others bow their heads in prayer and ask God to restore Mejal's equilibrium.

Mejal rocks on her milk pail. Then she tumbles off it and lies in the straw, her body quite rigid.

Salome lies down beside her and continues to whisper inaudibly into her ear and to hold her. The women pray.

Agata says: Almighty Father, in all humility and supplication we ask Thee for Thy abundant kindness this moment. We beseech Thee, have mercy on our sister Mejal. Please, in your beneficence, heal her. Please, we ask of Thee, envelop her in your strength and everlasting love, and please drive out the sickness that afflicts her now.

The women continue to bow their heads and to offer various words of praise to our heavenly Father. (I remember how my father, two days before he disappeared, told me that the twin pillars that guard the entrance to the shrine of religion are storytelling and cruelty.)

Salome very discreetly covers Mejal's ears to the prayers of the women.

Now Salome has asked Ona to roll Mejal a smoke. She continues to whisper, inaudibly, in Mejal's ear. Mejal appears stable now, less rigid. She has stopped shaking. Her breathing has returned to normal.

Ona has rolled Mejal a smoke, which she offers to her, with apologies. She is not an experienced cigarette maker; she frowns at its shape.

The other women continue praying, their heads bowed, each holding the other's hand.

Mejal recovers and both she and Salome return to their places at the table.

Agata says: Praise be to God.

Greta asks Autje to run out to the pump for water, to prepare cups of instant coffee, and Autje flies from the table. Neitje instantly follows, like a barn swallow. They are gone.

Salome runs to the window and calls Neitje back to the loft.

We hear Neitje yelling from a distance, No, why? I'm helping Autje!

Let her be, says Agata.

But Salome calls once more to Neitje, and then is silent, watching out the window.

Neitje returns to the loft.

Agata is visibly upset with Salome, but holds her peace.

Mariche now declares that Mejal's episode was brought on by the thought of the women creating their own map. Not a conscious fear of do-it-yourself map-making, she explains, but of what it implies: that we are masters of our own destiny. That we will be setting off into unknowable space.

Yes, says Agata, it stands to reason that one would panic . . .

Mejal blows smoke rings. I am not panicking, she says.

Yes, says Agata. But panic, in this case, *would* be understandable.

But I'm not, says Mejal.

Agata glances at the ceiling.

After a brief silence, Greta regales the women, now, with an anecdote. For three years, she says, she could only walk backwards, never forwards, due to an injury sustained to her groin. (I glean that the idea of setting off without knowing where you were going contributed to this memory.)

Soon another incident is upon us, distracting Mejal from her discomfort with the unknown.

Nettie (Melvin) Gerbrandt is once again climbing the ladder to the loft, this time carrying Mariche's youngest son, Julius Loewen, who appears to be inconsolable.

Greta raises her arms into the air. What in heaven's name?

Nettie (who, since the attacks, as I have pointed out, speaks only to children) thrusts small Julius into Mariche's lap. She gesticulates, pointing to the boy's nose and expressing, as far as I can decipher, bewilderment.

Agata calmly asks if Nettie might make an exception, and please be reasonable and speak to these circumstances. There are only women here in the loft, she points out. (I remain very still.)

Nettie is silent, pondering Agata's request, while Julius howls in Mariche's arms.

What has happened to him? Mariche asks urgently, above the din.

Nettie, says Agata. Be realistic. What has happened to Julius?

At last, Nettie speaks, but faces Julius as she does so. She says that young Julius has put a cherry pit into his nostril and that she is unable to remove it without pushing it further and further up into his nose.

At once, the women react. They are once again speaking over each other and I am unable to record the minutes.

Ona inserts two fingers into her mouth and whistles. (What a charming skill! And practical asset.)

The other women stop talking and look at her.

There are two faint vertical creases between Ona's eyes, tiny railroad tracks that lead up towards her hairline but disappear halfway there. If Julius has put a cherry pit into his nose, she says, then it follows that Julius has been eating cherries or certainly has been in the proximity of cherries. We have no cherries in Molotschna. The cherries that we eat are always brought from the city, as a treat for the members of the colony, by one of the elders who has been to the city on business.

The women are silent, absorbing this news. Agata steadies her gaze and is still.

Salome, cursing, goes to the window.

Greta calls down to Autje, who has not quite reached the loft ladder on her way back from the pump. Find out if some of the men have already returned from the city, she says. And if they have, try to find out which men they are.

Also, she hollers down, if the men ask where their womenfolk are, tell them that Ruth and Cheryl are foaling late this spring and there are problems!

At this, Agata objects. The men of the colony know that Ruth and Cheryl were not bred last year, she points out, so could not be expected to foal this spring. She hollers down at Autje: Tell the men, if they ask, that their womenfolk are attending the difficult birth of their sister, in labour, in Chortiza!

This is met with approval from the other women. No man from Molotschna Colony will interfere with (or express interest in) childbirth, especially all the way over in Chortiza.

Agata also asks Autje to put her kerchief back on. Autje and Neitje have both tied their kerchiefs jauntily around their wrists, the fashion for the Molotschna teenagers when men are not present.

Mariche now takes a turn hollering at her daughter: Tell the men that we are quilting, but say you don't know in whose house, and that we must continue well into the night as there has been a late and large order from the co-op!

A note of explanation: The co-op sells Mennonite goods to tourists. The women of Molotschna provide the goods, but are forbidden to visit the co-op or to handle the money from the sales.

Ah, Salome says, that's a good one. No man of Molotschna will be seen in the vicinity of a ladies' quilting circle. She is standing at the window, watching Autje: There she goes, running.

Salome turns away from the window to face the women. She says to Neitje, You must run now to every house and tell the women to tell the men, if they encounter them and if the men ask, that some of us are working late into the night to finish the quilting order, and that others of us are attending to the difficult birth of one of our sisters in Chortiza. The men will want to eat. Remind the women to tell the men, if they are the menfolk of any of us here in this loft, that we have left containers of soup and loaves of bread in the larders. The men will leave again in the morning and will understand that we are working at these various things all night long and won't be available to see them off.

Neitje doesn't move immediately.

Salome prods her, Go, go!

Neitje languidly gets up from her pail, in silence, stretching first, fixing her hair until Salome is apoplectic and barks her name, Neitje!

By now Mariche has successfully removed the cherry pit from Julius's nose, using her mouth to suction it out as one would to remove venom from a snake bite, or to siphon gas illicitly from a police vehicle, and Julius is happily chewing on a rotten piece of leather from an old bridle once belonging to Earnest Thiessen's team. Agata informs Nettie that she is free to go, and should return to the other children. Julius will remain in the loft for the time being.

But Mariche asks Nettie to stay for a minute. How did Julius come into the possession of cherries? she asks.

Then she asks, Was it Klaas? (Mariche's own husband.)

Nettie answers, again speaking to Julius, looking only at him while he plays and chews, oblivious. She explains that Julius and a few of the older children were in the yard, and that one of the children spotted the buggy on the mile road, and that this older child, likely Benny Eidse, encouraged the others, including Julius, who rode on the shoulders of one of the stronger children, to go and meet the buggy. When they returned they had a paper sack of cherries that they were passing around, sharing, and Julius was afflicted with the pit.

Mariche asks Nettie: So you don't know who was in the buggy?

Nettie speaks to Julius: I do not.

Mejal says, I am worried about the women who have voted to do nothing (in response to the attacks). If the men have returned, there is a high risk that these women will inform the men that we are plotting this insurrection.

Mariche scoffs. It's not an insurrection, that is not the correct word.

Salome sighs, exasperated. Mariche, you continuously sabotage our meetings by positioning yourself as the authority on something, anything, always something arbitrary and ridiculous. And if you counter no opposition, you insist you are right. And you become hysterical when you are challenged.

No, Mariche interrupts. It is you, Salome, or maybe some other Friesen woman present, who is always extolling the glory of precise, accurate language, of using the correct word. And in this case the word "insurrection" is blatantly incorrect because insurrections involve violence, and what we women of Molotschna are planning does *not* include violence.

Ona beseeches the women to remain calm. Our meeting must proceed, she says. And Mariche is correct. "Insurrection" is not the right word to describe our plan. We will name it properly when we have the details in place.

She returns to Mejal's earlier point, about the risk of the Do Nothing women informing on us to the men. It's true, she says, that these women will refuse to commit the sin of lying. We will simply have to have faith that these women, to remain innocent of prevarication, will plead ignorance if asked about our whereabouts, or that they will creatively, though piously, evade the question altogether.

(I force myself not to speak to this point, not to chastise, not to challenge, not to haughtily disabuse Ona of her trust, not to give any single indication that I am concerned about betrayal, about dark hearts, about Scarface Janz in particular. And I beg God, silently, to forgive me my trespasses, my suspicions, and to imbue me with the same faith that Ona has in her sister colonists, in all of us, in goodness.)

Ona goes on to say that she is concerned that the men who have returned temporarily to Molotschna will take horses and/or livestock that the women will later need, either to sell or to provide support along the way.

Mariche asks: Along the way? I was not aware that we have made a final decision about staying or leaving. The only thing I'm aware of having decided is that the women are not animals. And even that conclusion was arrived at without solid consensus amongst the women.

Yes, Ona admits, it is true that we haven't fully made a decision to leave. But if we do leave we will need as many animals as we can get.

How can we prevent the men from taking some of the animals, Greta asks Ona, considering that this is the only reason the men have returned in the first place?

Ona has a suggestion: perhaps through Nettie (who is lingering still in the hayloft) we could convey the message that the animals have taken sick since the men first departed for the city and that they have been quarantined?

Mejal reminds Ona that Nettie does not speak to adults.

Mariche points out that the story of the quarantine is yet another lie, a profound transgression. Not only have we committed the sin of lying, she says, we have tutored our daughters to do the same. If we spur Nettie on to lie as well, we'll be guilty of taking advantage of a dummkopf.

Salome raises her hand. Nettie is not a "dummkopf," she declares. Nettie's unusual behaviour—giving herself a boy's name and speaking only to children—is an understandable response to the prolonged and especially horrific attack she endured.

We are all victims, says Mariche.

True, Salome says, but our responses are varied and one is not more or less appropriate than the other.

Mariche waves this objection away. She continues to expound her thesis on lying. Surely, she says, encouraging others to lie on our behalves must be a worse sin than lying ourselves. And how will we be forgiven for this lie (about the whereabouts of the women, quilting, attending to childbirth, etc.) if not by the elders whom we have lied against, and whom, if our plan to leave becomes a reality, we will never see again, therefore leaving us unforgiven, bereft of mercy, with black hearts, and unable to enter the kingdom of God?

Perhaps, says Greta, there will be other elders or men of God that will be able to forgive us our sins, individuals we have not yet met.

At this, Salome erupts. She raises her voice, causing Miep to awaken and Julius to stop chewing on the leather. We do not have to be forgiven by the men of God, she shouts, for protecting our children from the depraved actions of vicious men who are often the very same men we are meant to ask for forgiveness. If God is a loving God He will forgive us Himself. If God is a vengeful God then He has created us in His image. If God is omnipotent then why has He not protected the women and girls of Molotschna? If God, in the book of Matthew, according to Peters, our wise bishop, asks: Let the children come to me and do not hinder them, then mustn't we consider it a hindrance when our children are attacked?

Salome pauses, perhaps to rest . . .

No, not to rest. Salome continues to shout: She will destroy any living thing that harms her child, she will tear it from limb to limb, she will desecrate its body and she will bury it alive. She will challenge God on the spot to strike her dead if she has sinned by protecting her child from evil, and furthermore by destroying the evil that it may not harm another. She will lie, she will hunt, she will kill and she will dance on graves and burn forever in hell before she allows another man to satisfy his violent urges with the body of her three-year-old child.

No, says Agata softly, not dancing. Not desecration.

Miep has begun to cry and little Julius is laughing, unsure of himself, eyes shining, tiny pearls.

Mejal goes to Salome, as Salome went to Mejal earlier, and takes Salome into her arms.

Ona picks Miep from the straw and sings to her, a song about ducks. (Does Ona remember the happiness and consolation I feel when I hear the sounds ducks make?)

Agata, aside from whispering to Nettie to return now to the other children, is silent. Greta and Mariche, too, are quite silent.

Nettie climbs down the loft ladder.

Ona's voice is all we/I hear. She is playful as she sings, speeding up the lyrics as the fish winnow and race, slowing them down as the fish bask in the sunlight close to the surface of the water. The children are calm, enthralled. Ona continues to sing the song about ducks swimming in the sea, one, two, three and four.

Ona asks the children if they know what a sea is, and they stare at her with four enormous blue eyes, sea-like. Ona describes the sea as another world, one that is hidden from us, one that lives underwater. It is the life in the sea that she defines as the sea, and not the sea itself. She talks about fish and other living things.

At last, Mariche interrupts. The sea is a vast expanse of water, and nothing else, she tells the children. They're children, Ona, she explains. How can they be expected to understand what goes on invisibly? Besides, you have never seen a sea.

Salome begins to laugh. She says: The life underwater is not invisible. It isn't unable to be seen. We just can't see it from here. My God.

You are ignorant of a child's sensibilities, Salome, says Mariche.

Oh, says Salome, am I? If I allowed my child to be beaten black and blue by a shit for brains, like your Klaas, would I be considered less ignorant of how a child perceives a hidden life?

Mariche is silent, shocked.

Salome, says Mejal, that doesn't make any sense. She advises Salome to have a drag from her cigarette.

Ona agrees, silently. I know that she thinks Salome's attack was unclear and beneath her. I know it because she looked at Salome and furrowed her brow in a way that I witnessed earlier (the disappearing rail tracks that line her forehead). Overall, Ona is tolerant of her sister's rages and circumspect in her response to them. Perhaps she has learned over the years that no good comes from crossing her younger sibling.

As if reading my thoughts, Agata now suggests that we *think* of what is good. She recites a verse from Philippians: Whatever is true, whatever is honourable, whatever is just, whatever is pure, whatever is pleasing, whatever is commendable, if there is any excellence and if there is anything worthy of praise, think about these things . . . and the peace of God be with you.

The other women wait for each other to speak first,

to answer Agata's call for suggestions of goodness. In truth, the women seem not to be actively engaged in this endeavour.

Salome bypasses the question altogether. I will become a murderer if I stay, she says to her mother. (I assume that she means if she stays in the colony, and is here when and if the captured men are granted bail and return home from the city.)

What is worse than that? Salome asks Agata.

Agata nods. She continues to nod. Her lips are pursed and she is blinking and nodding. The heels of her hands rest on the table but her fingers are vertical, reaching towards the beams of the hayloft, towards God, towards meaning. The other women do not speak. Unusual.

I have seen Michelangelo's *The Creation of Adam* in a book of famous paintings left at the co-op by a Swiss tourist. The book was passed around the colony discreetly, by my father, but Peters Senior eventually discovered it and destroyed it. Rumour has it that he tore out every page and lit them on fire one by one—if only for the opportunity to lay his eyes on all the paintings. A busier man with clearer intentions would have ignited the thing in one go and tossed it into the fire bin.

The women are still eerily silent.

I only mention the book of famous paintings because of Agata's fingers pointing towards God. This reminds me, in a way, of *The Creation of Adam*. And because it is silent in the hayloft and I want to appear to be industrious and my job here is to write—this is something to write, my first thought.

The women remain silent, thinking about what is good, just, pleasing, pure, etc. Or perhaps about other things. I don't know what they are thinking. About arson, perhaps. I'm reminded, by thinking of *The Creation of Adam*, of another fact about human fingers.

Human fingers can feel objects as small as thirteen nanometres, which means that if your finger was the size of the earth you could feel the difference between a barn and a horse. I want to remember to mention this to Ona. I want to mention, too, Michelangelo's *The Creation of Eve* (the fifth panel of the Sistine Chapel work), which is not nearly as well-known or as popular a painting as *The Creation of Adam*. In *The Creation of Eve*, Adam lies passed out on a stone and Eve is standing, naked, begging to God for something. What could it be? God has come down to earth in this painting, no longer drifting around on a cloud and casually reaching out His finger. This time God looks stern, intense. He has come to earth to speak to Eve . . . or has He come at her request? Why has He left his cloud of cherubs?

In the painting, Eve is beseeching God, begging, imploring . . . perhaps reasoning, as though she has it within her power to restore Christianity to its original grandeur. She's working behind the back of Adam, who is sleeping on the ground, as if to suggest that she knows he'd disapprove. But disapprove of what? Of her meeting privately with God? Or of what she is saying?

Another fact regarding the co-op: There is a faded photograph tacked to the south-facing wall. It is a photo-graph published by *The Guardian* newspaper in England,

and it was snapped by a professional photographer who had come to Molotschna, many years ago, to look at Mennonites. It was this photographer who first mentioned the idea of England to my father. The photograph depicts several young men and women from our colony. The caption beneath the photograph reads: *Mennonites like to spend some time chatting under the stars before going to sleep.*

In the photograph, taken at night, we see Mennonite girls sitting outside in plastic chairs in the darkness under an eminently starry night. It appears as though something cataclysmic, and yet unnoticed, has just occurred above these chatting Mennonites. The sky is beginning to turn a mustardy yellow. There are two men in the background, talking. And there are two buggies and two horses. There is a house and a tree and a silo. One of the women in the photograph is Ona. She's slim, young, leaning forward to hear what the other girls are saying. Her long fingers are clutching the armrests of the plastic chair she's sitting in as though she's prepared to launch forward at any moment, or perhaps to shoot up into the yellow sky above her.

Ona has not seen this photograph, of course, but someday I would like to tell her about it. After the attacks there were many photographers from all over the world stopping in at the co-op asking for directions to the colony. Peters decreed that no one at the co-op would speak to these individuals. Heinz Gerbrandt, a blacksmith whose forge is next to the co-op, told me in church that a newspaper clipping from an American newspaper had been mailed to the co-op. It had originally been dropped off at his forge because the door to the co-op was locked. Heinz

Gerbrandt walked with the letter to the co-op. He remembered holding it away from his body, like something hot, dangerous. The headline read: *In 2009 the Devil Appeared, in the Shape of Seven Ghosts, to the Girls and Women of the Molotschna Colony.* Heinz Gerbrandt told me that Peters, upon discovering this clipping, had nodded his head in agreement. Yes, he had said, according to Heinz Gerbrandt. That is true. "Dump men in the middle of nowhere, confine them, abuse them, suspend them in limbo, and this is what you get."

I asked Heinz Gerbrandt if Peters had really said that? And Heinz confirmed it. Heinz told me that this is what Peters had said to him, with tears in his eyes, while the two of them were re-shingling the church roof.

But then how can he carry on here as the bishop of Molotschna, the way he does? I asked Heinz.

Heinz shook his head. He didn't know. He suggested we analyze the statement: "Dump men in the middle of nowhere, confine them, abuse them, suspend them in limbo, and this is what you get."

Heinz and I stood on the road that leads out of Molotschna, towards the border, and whispered these words over and over, trying to come to an understanding of what Peters meant. Or, of why he had said them with tears in his eyes. Or, of why he had said them.

Heinz Gerbrandt has left Molotschna. He took his wife and children with him. It is said that he became frightened after hearing Peters say it was true that the devil had visited the girls and women of Molotschna. It is said that Heinz Gerbrandt is not enough of a man or believer to accept the truth. It is said that Heinz Gerbrandt is easily discouraged and that the world will shatter him. Peters has officially excommunicated Heinz Gerbrandt, but everyone knows that ruling is weak as Heinz Gerbrandt left the church and the colony of his own initiative.

Heinz Gerbrandt gave me a gift once, of a horseshoe. They are said to bring luck, he said. In Molotschna luck does not exist. It is a sin to believe in luck. It is shameful to cry. All is God's will, nothing is left to chance in God's creation. If God created the world, why should we not be in it?

I will remember Heinz Gerbrandt.

The women remain silent. Ona has come to where I am sitting and is looking over my shoulder. Will she put her hand on my shoulder? She is looking at me while I write. My pen is shaking. She can't read, so I could write the words, *Ona, my soul belongs to you*, and she would not know.

She breaks the silence. August, she says, I know what these are (she points at the letters). They are letters. But what are these little things?

I tell her that they are commas, that they signify a short pause, or a breath, in the text.

Ona smiles, then inhales, as if to take back her words, to take them back inside her body, perhaps to give to her unborn child words, the narrative, hers . . . she says nothing more and I struggle to respond in some way.

Did you know, I say, that there is a butterfly called the Comma?

Ona gasps.

It's such an untoward reaction, so comical.

Is that so? she asks.

Yes, I say, it's called the Comma because—but Ona stops me.

No, she says, let me guess. Because it flits about from leaf to stem to petal, pausing only briefly on its way? Because its journey is its story, never stopping, only pausing, always moving.

I smile and nod. Exactly, I say, that is why!

Ona punches the palm of her hand: Aha! She goes back to her seat.

But it's not true, this is not why the Comma butterfly has its name. And of course there are periods within texts, journeys. Stoppage. The real reason, banal, is that the butterfly has a shape on the underside of its wing that resembles a comma.

I don't know now why I let her believe otherwise, but someday, perhaps, it will be clear.

Ah, the women are stirring, this reverie has ended. I will resume taking the minutes.

Agata speaks.

Salome, she says, there is nothing worse than being a murderer. If you will become a murderer by staying in the colony, side by side with the men who are responsible for the attacks and side by side with the men who are posting enough bail to have the attackers return to the colony while they await trial, then you must, to protect your own soul and to qualify for entry into heaven, leave the colony.

Mariche frowns, unhappy with Agata's reasoning. We are not all murderers, she objects.

Not yet, says Ona.

Agata nods. Mariche, she says, have you ever considered killing one of or all the men responsible for the attacks?

Never, says Mariche. What *dummheit*.

Have you ever wished the attackers dead? asks Agata.

Mariche concedes that she has, but instantly asked God to forgive her.

And do you believe your murderous thoughts would multiply if the men were in your vicinity? Agata persists. If you were to see the men every day, and if the men were in a position of authority over you and your children, and it was expected of you, by Peters, to obey these men?

Yes, says Mariche, I believe that would be the case, that my murderous thoughts would multiply under those conditions.

Ah, says Salome, so you do have murderous thoughts.

No, says Mariche, I told you. I only wish the men were dead.

And that is why we must leave, concludes Agata.

Some of the women, including Mariche and Greta, open their mouths to object, and Greta raises her arms in the air.

But Agata continues: I have done what the verse from Philippians instructed, which is to think about what is good, what is just, what is pure, and what is excellent. And I have arrived at an answer: pacifism.

Pacifism, Agata says, is good. Any violence is unjustifiable. By staying in Molotschna, she says, we women would be betraying the central tenet of the Mennonite faith, which is pacifism, because by staying we would knowingly be placing ourselves in a direct collision course with violence, perpetrated by us or against us. We would be inviting harm. We would be in a state of war. We would turn Molotschna into a battlefield. By staying in Molotschna we would be bad Mennonites. We would be sinners, according to our faith, and we would be denied entry to heaven.

Mejal takes a long haul off her cigarette. She exhales, and nods. Agata is right.

Let's shake a leg, then, Mejal says.

But by staying and fighting, Mariche objects, we will hopefully achieve peace for our children. Eventually. And our colony will remain intact and we will remain apart from the world, not in the world, which is another central tenet of our Mennonite faith.

That's true, says Agata, but there is no tenet within our faith that demands we stay apart from the world together with men who inspire violence in our hearts and minds.

Ona asks Mariche, Do you really mean that you want to stay and NOT fight? Because when was the last time you had the strength to stand up to the aggression of Klaas, to protect your children, or to get out of harm's way?

Mariche is enraged. She rises, her jaw set, her eyes scorching. Who are you, she demands of Ona, to tell me what kind of a wife and mother to be when you are neither one yourself? Who are you but a dreamer, an idiot savant, a spinster, a crazy woman cursed with Narfa, a lunatic!

I'm writing as fast as I can but I cannot keep up with Mariche. She has called Ona a whore, an unwed mother.

Salome has risen now from her milk bucket. She is yelling at Mariche. She says that Ona was made unconscious and raped, like so many others, and now is with child as a result. How dare Mariche call Ona a whore. God, in His creation of the world, forced Adam into a deep sleep and while he was sleeping God removed one of his ribs and from that rib he created Eve. Was Adam a whore?

Mariche hollers back, Adam was a man!

Salome ignores her, shouting: Did Adam initiate that act himself? Was he able to protect himself?

(As a quick aside, for later thought: I'm curious about Salome's comment, considering the coincidental note I made in my notebook earlier referring to Michelangelo's painting.)

Salome continues to yell, her voice hoarse. Mariche, are you not afraid that your own sweet Julius will become a monster like his father because you do nothing to protect him, nothing to educate him, nothing to teach him the criminality of his father's ways, the depravity . . .

Agata hobbles (her edema is still an issue) to where Salome is standing. She gently urges her daughter back onto the milk bucket and strokes her hair, murmuring words I can't make out. Agata strokes Salome's hair with one hand and rubs her own eyes with her other hand, an action that makes clicking sounds.

Salome gently pulls Agata's hand away from her mother's eyes. Don't, she says. That sound. You're rubbing them too hard.

Agata smiles. The tenderness.

Salome is insane, says Mariche. She has stopped making sense.

Mariche adds, turning to face Ona: How dare you pass judgement on me?

Ona meets Mariche's gaze and smiles. It wasn't judgement, she says, it was a question.

Agata leans over to whisper to Ona.

Ona apologizes to Mariche, who suggests that Ona engage in a crude activity I cannot mention. (I'll mention here that Mariche, in broken English, also told Ona to "fuck it off." So much of what exists in the outside world is kept out of Molotschna, but curses, like pain, always find a way in.)

Mariche! Greta says. Sit down and be quiet.

Mariche sits down loudly.

Mejal and Salome are sharing a cigarette—waiting, it seems, for the air to clear.

Agata continues to stroke Salome's arms and hair. She is rubbing her own eyes again, and they are making the little clicking sounds.

Salome frowns and says again, Mother, don't.

Mariche is silent.

Neitje whispers: It's "fuck off," I think. The others nod in agreement.

Ona apologizes again and adds that she, too, was considering the verse from Philippians and thinking on what is good. Freedom is good, she says. It's better than slavery. And forgiveness is good, better than revenge. And hope for the unknown is good, better than hatred of the familiar.

Mariche remains strangely calm. She asks Ona, genuinely and without sarcasm, But what about security, safety, home and family? What about the sanctity of marriage, of obedience, of love?

I don't know about those things, any of them, says Ona. Except for love. And even love, she says, is mysterious to me. And I believe that my home is with my mother, with my sister and with my unborn child, wherever they may be.

Mariche asks: Will you not hate your unborn child, because he or she is the child of a man who inspires violent thoughts in you?

I already love this child more than anything, Ona says. He or she is as innocent and loveable as the evening sun—

She looks at me. I hold my breath and scratch my head, plead for forgiveness, but for what, or for whom, oh this temporal light—

And so, too, says Ona, was the child's father when he was born.

Wait, says Mejal, I disagree. That man was born evil. God brought him into this world to test us, to test our faith.

Salome scoffs. Wasn't it you, Mejal, who months ago said all the attackers were employed by the devil? So which one is it? Are God and the devil one and the same to you?

Mejal rolls her eyes and says, Oh, fuck it, I don't know.

I do not want to hear that language anymore, Greta says wearily.

Agata makes a small noise. Is she crying? No, she isn't crying. She has rubbed her eyes too hard, just like Salome said she would, and has hurt herself.

Mariche continues her queries, still calm. If Ona is saying that forgiveness is good, better than revenge, is she implying that we must forgive the men of Molotschna, particularly the attackers, rather than serve justice by retaliating? And if so, wouldn't it be possible to stay in Molotschna, and forgive the men?

But the men of Molotschna, and particularly the attackers, have not asked for forgiveness, Salome points out.

Yes, says Mariche, but Peters will insist that the attackers ask for forgiveness. And then, so as not to sin against God and risk being excommunicated and exiled, we will have to forgive them!

Greta has now laid her head on the table next to her teeth. (A small rodent, the same one or a different one from before, is crossing the floor of the loft. Why are there so many of you and where are you going?)

Forgiveness is moot, Ona insists, if not heartfelt. The only thing we must do is protect our God-given souls. We must find it in our own hearts to forgive the men of Molotschna, regardless of what Peters or anybody else expects of us and even if the men don't ask for it them-selves and even if they claim their innocence all the way to their graves.

So, you believe that maintaining the condition of your own soul is more important than obeying God? Mariche says, less calm now.

They are the same thing, really, Ona says, steadily. I believe that my soul, my essence, my intangible energy, is the presence of God within me, and that by bringing peace to my soul I am honouring God. If I can understand how these crimes may have occurred I am able to forgive these men. And I am almost able, certainly from a distance, to pity these men, and to love them. Love is good, and better than retaliation.

Mariche rises to her feet once again. Ona is preposterous, she rages. Everything she says is ridiculous, blasphemous and morally corrupt.

Greta, weary, lifts her head and then her arms, although not as high as before. Again, she beseeches Mariche to sit down.

Agata speaks: Ona, she says, you make a good point. You mention that certainly from a distance these things are possible: forgiveness, compassion and love. And that adherence to our Mennonite faith requires these things of us. And so, really, we must leave in order to achieve that distance you speak of. Perhaps we could call it perspective. A new perspective, one that is rational, understanding AND loving and obedient, and in keeping with our faith, all at the same time. It is our duty to leave. Would you agree? That the word is "perspective," and that we would possess this with some distance?

Not fighting, but moving on, says Ona. Always moving. Never fighting. Just moving. Always moving. She seems to be in some kind of trance.

Mariche tells Ona to snap out of it.

You snap out of it, Mariche, says Salome.

All of you snap out of it and focus, Mejal says. Have you lost your minds? She jabs at the window, at the sun outside, at its passing.

Greta, sitting fully upright now, tells us a new story about her team, Ruth and Cheryl.

Several of the women groan, but she ignores this.

In the past, Greta says, she had always been frightened of the road between Molotschna and Chortiza. It is so narrow and the gullies on either side of the road are so deep. It was only when she learned to focus her gaze far ahead of her, down the road, and not on the road immediately in front of her team that she felt safe. Before she learned to do this, says Greta, her buggy would weave and lurch perilously from side to side. Ruth and Cheryl were simply following her commands on the reins, but her commands were reckless, jerky, frenetic and dangerous. Leaving will give us the more far-seeing perspective we need to forgive, which is to love properly, and to keep the peace, according to our faith. Therefore, our leaving wouldn't be an act of cowardice, abandonment, disobedience or rebellion. It wouldn't be because we were excommunicated or exiled. It would be a supreme act of faith. And of faith in God's abiding goodness.

And the fact that we would be breaking up our families? asks Mariche. Taking our children away from their fathers?

Our duty is to God. (Agata)

Precisely—to our souls, which are the manifestation of God. (Ona)

Ona, let me finish. (Agata) Our duty is to protect the creatures He has created, which is ourselves and our children, and to bear witness to our faith. Our faith requires of us absolute commitment to pacifism, love and forgiveness. By staying, we risk these things. We will be at war with our attackers because we've acknowledged that we—well, some of us—want to kill them. The only forgiveness we can offer if we stay would be coerced and not genuine. By leaving we will sooner achieve those things required of us by our faith—pacifism, love and forgiveness. And we will be teaching our children that these are our values. By leaving we will be teaching our children that they must pursue these values above and beyond the expectations of their fathers.

Is that blasphemous? insists Mariche.

The others are silent.

Okay, so we leave, Mariche continues. And then, morally? We're unimpeachable? We've acted according to God's will. But what happens when we become hungry? Or afraid?

Hunger and fear, Ona objects, are the things we share with animals. Can the fear of hunger and fear be our guide?

Mariche frowns at Ona. What are you talking about? Surely we need to think about hunger and fear.

Mejal raises her hand.

Just speak, says Greta. She looks exhausted and pale.

Mejal tactfully brings up Ruth and Cheryl. Would the horses have themselves extended their vision, and looked far down the road rather than myopically, if not for the commanding human pressure on the reins? Would the horses have understood how not to fall into the gully without the direction of a human hand?

Why are you asking? interjects Salome. Are you suggesting that if we follow our innate animal instincts, and act on fear and hunger or on the fear of falling, we'll somehow find perspective and achieve peace?

Mejal yawns. I was only wondering, only thinking out loud, she says.

But Salome won't drop the thread. It is true that hunger and fear are the things we share with animals, as Ona pointed out, not the intelligence that allows us to establish perspective or distance in order to better assess a situation.

No, says Mariche, that's not true either. Animals, and even insects, are perfectly capable of perspective. Didn't Ona herself mention the long-term planning abilities of dragonflies? How they are able to set out on a course of action knowing, or if not knowing then instinctively understanding, that they would not see the end of their journey but their offspring would?

Well, says Salome, we don't know what dragonflies are thinking, or if they think. I'm not sure that's what you would call perspective.

Why shouldn't I? asks Mariche.

Because it may not be the correct word, says Salome.

What difference does that make? asks Mariche.

Every difference, says Salome.

Mariche suddenly changes the subject, and turns to me. She asks me what I was writing before, when the women were silent. And why I was writing at all, if my job is to translate what the women are saying into English and record those words on paper?

I have answered (startled and embarrassed) that I'm not sure what she's referring to.

But Mariche is not satisfied. Before, she says, you were writing things, but we weren't talking. So what were you writing?

I have responded: I was writing about a photograph I've seen at the co-op and about a painting by Michelangelo.

Mariche nods—with approval? Reproach? (Ah, reproach.)

Runs in the family, she says.

Mejal asks me: What photograph?

I don't know how to answer.

Ona speaks, rescuing me yet again. It has just occurred to her, she says, that the women could consider another option, besides leaving and besides staying and fighting and besides doing nothing.

Mariche reminds her that it's late in the day to introduce another option. Greta waves this comment away and gestures to Ona to speak.

We could ask the men to leave, says Ona.

Is that a joke? asks Mariche.

Salome, unexpectedly, agrees with Mariche. Are you crazy, Ona? she asks.

Perhaps all of us are crazy, Ona says.

Of course we're all crazy, says Mejal. How can we not be?

(I'd like to return to this comment later, but for now must hurry along.)

Agata ignores the talk of craziness and returns to Ona's original question: We ask the men to leave? You mean the attackers and the elders who support their return?

And Peters, of course, says Ona.

Greta lifts her arm. Untenable, she says. Imagine the response of the men, upon being asked to leave the colony. What reason would be given to them?

Everything we've discussed, says Ona. That to uphold the charter of our faith we must engage in pacifism, in love and forgiveness. That to be near these men hardens our hearts towards them and generates feelings of hatred and violence. That if we are to continue (or return to) being Good Mennonites, we must separate the men from the women until we can discover (or rediscover) our righteous path.

But, says Mariche, how are the boys and men of Molotschna expected to relearn their habits and their treatment of girls and women if there are no girls or women left in the colony to practise on! By leaving, she continues, we are removing the possibility of re-education for our boys and men. That's irresponsible.

Ona pauses. She makes round shapes with her hands, as though they contain the universe.

Mariche, she says, you have, interestingly, made a relevant point.

Please do not imply that my other points weren't interesting by claiming this one to be, says Mariche.

Ona laughs. I didn't mean that, she says.

Salome interrupts. It's not our responsibility to educate the boys and men of Molotschna, she says. Let August do it. (!)

But perhaps it *is* our responsibility, counters Mejal. Especially if those boys are our sons, and if their fathers are incapable of doing the task themselves.

Greta states: Don't tell me we're considering staying in order to teach the boys and men of Molotschna how to behave like human beings! Will we put them in desks?

Agata (her hand once again on her chest) soothes the women. Nay, nay, she says.

Ona whispers, not *in* desks, *at* desks.

Salome laughs. We'll get out the strap, she says, and make them wear dunce's caps.

No, Salome, demurs Ona. That defeats the purpose of the teaching of non-violence.

Mejal asks: What are dunce's caps?

(On a personal note, I am on tenterhooks, hoping Ona doesn't reintroduce the subject of Mariche's own son, Julius, and the risk of him becoming an attacker if he isn't taught differently. Mariche's anger with Ona is now a tinderbox. Explosive.)

Greta grimaces and moves her hand slowly in front of her face. I am sorry, she tells the other women, but I think I might be dying.

Some of the women rise, in alarm, from their seats.

Mariche looks directly into Greta's eyes. Then she laughs. She removes Greta's eyeglasses and asks the other women to look at them. Mother, she says, you are not dying. Your glasses need cleaning.

Greta, mightily relieved, laughs, exclaiming that she thought the lights were going out.

Agata hoots. That would alter your perspective! she says.

The women laugh and laugh. Agata struggles for breath. The youngsters (Miep and Julius), startled by the noise, return to their mothers' laps. They've been playing, constructing a miniature barn with animals made from straw and manure.

The sun is setting, Ona reminds us, and our light is fading. We should light the kerosene lamp.

But what of your question? asks Greta. Should we consider asking the men to leave?

None of us have ever asked the men for anything, Agata states. Not a single thing, not even for the salt to be passed, not even for a penny or a moment alone or to take the washing in or to open a curtain or to go easy on the small yearlings or to put your hand on the small of my back as I try, again, for the twelfth or thirteenth time, to push a baby out of my body.

Isn't it interesting, she says, that the one and only request the women would make of the men would be to leave?

The women break out laughing again.

They simply can't stop laughing, and if one of them stops for a moment she will quickly resume laughing with a loud burst, and off they'll all go again.

It's not an option, says Agata, at last.

No, the others (finally in complete accord!) agree. Asking the men to leave is not an option.

Greta asks the women to imagine her team, Ruth and Cheryl (Agata yelps in exasperation at the mention of their names), requesting that Greta leave them alone for the day to graze in the field and do nothing.

Imagine my hens, adds Agata, telling me to turn around and leave the premises when I show up to gather the eggs.

Ona begs the women to stop making her laugh, she's afraid she'll go into premature labour.

This makes them laugh harder! They even find it uproariously funny that I continue to write during all of this. Ona's laughter is the finest, the most exquisite sound in all of nature, filled with breath and promise, and the only sound she releases into the world that she doesn't also try to retrieve.

Agata slaps me on the back. She rubs her eyes again, making them click, but I can see this time they are filled with tears of laughter.

You must think we're all lunatics, she says.

I insist that I don't, and nor does it matter what I think.

Ona stops laughing, barely. Do you think that's true, she asks, that it doesn't matter what you think?

I blush. Maul my own head.

She continues: How would you feel if in your entire lifetime it had never mattered what you thought?

But I'm not here to think, I answer, I'm here to take the minutes of your meeting.

Ona brushes my words aside. But if, in all your life, she says, you truly felt that it didn't matter what you thought, how would that make you feel?

I smile and mutter something about God's will being my purpose.

Ona smiles back (!). But how are we to determine God's will, if not by thinking?

I blush again and shake my head, resist the urge to claw it to pieces.

Salome interrupts: That's easy, Ona, Peters will interpret it for us!

The women howl with laughter yet again.

I am laughing too. I put down my pen.

The laughter fades. I don't know where to look or where to put my hands. I have arranged my pens and notebooks at right angles to each other.

Ona tells the women how itchy her stomach is, how she's afraid her skin won't stretch any further without tearing. The women laugh yet again, and Agata nearly falls off her milk pail.

I paused in my writing to put my hand on her shoulder for a moment. What a relief it was to have something to do with at least one of my hands, if only for a second.

The women are offering advice to Ona having to do with lard, sunflower oil, sunlight, clay and prayer. But something else has occurred to Ona. What if the men who have been imprisoned are not guilty? she asks.

But Leisl Neustadter caught one of them, says Neitje. Didn't she?

That's true, says Salome, she did. But only one. Gerhard Schellenberg. And he named his accomplices.

But what if he was lying? asks Ona.

Why would he lie? asks Greta.

Agata admonishes Greta: You're asking why a person who has no compunction about attacking children in their sleep would also lie about it? That's not a legitimate question.

Well, says Salome, it's legitimate, but possibly rhetorical. The men Gerhard named were also the men who showed up late in the morning for fieldwork, and were tired, with dark circles around their eyes.

That's only hearsay, conjecture, offers Ona. Just because you're late for work in the morning with dark circles around your eyes does not mean you've been up the night before sneaking into houses and attacking women.

But the point, says Salome (Mariche sighs, as if to say, *Here comes another one of Salome's finger-wagging points*), is that it makes no difference to whether or not we women leave Molotschna. We know that we've been attacked by men, or at least one man, Gerhard, and likely others, and not by ghosts or devils or Satan. We know that we have not imagined these attacks. And that we're not being punished by God for impure thoughts and deeds.

Mariche interrupts: Yet we've had impure thoughts, surely, haven't we?

The other women nod: Of course.

Salome ignores Mariche and continues. We know that we are bruised and infected and pregnant and terrified and insane and some of us are dead. We know that we must protect our children. We know that if these attacks continue our faith will be threatened because we will become angry, murderous and unforgiving. Regardless of who is guilty of them!

Alright, Salome, thank you, please sit down, says Agata. She tugs on Salome's sleeve.

I'd add, says Agata, that we have already also determined that we want to have time and space to think—

Salome interrupts: And that we want and need our *right* to think independently to be acknowledged, she says.

Or, says Mejal, just to think. Period. With or without it being acknowledged.

Yes, says Agata, and this is another reason for leaving Molotschna, but one that doesn't have anything to do directly with the attacks or the attackers.

But indirectly, most certainly, says Ona.

Salome, more calm now, adds: So once again, we return to our three reasons for leaving, and they are valid. We want our children to be safe. We want to keep our faith. And we want to think.

Agata splays her fingers on the plywood table as if to build a new foundation. Shall we move on? she asks.

But, says Mariche, if there is any chance that the men in prison are innocent shouldn't we, as members of Molotschna, be joining forces to secure their freedom?

Salome explodes. We're not *members* of Molotschna!

The other women recoil and even the sun takes shelter behind a cloud.

Greta, she says, are your beloved Ruth and Cheryl members of Molotschna?

No, not members, says Greta, although—

Salome interrupts. We're not *members*! she repeats. We are the *women* of Molotschna. The entire colony of Molotschna is built on the foundation of patriarchy (translator's note: Salome didn't use the word "patriarchy"—I inserted it in the place of Salome's curse, of mysterious origin, loosely translated as "talking through the flowers"), where the women live out their days as mute, submissive and obedient servants. Animals. Fourteen-year-old boys are expected to give us orders, to determine our fates, to vote on our excommunications, to speak at the burials of our own babies while we remain silent, to interpret the Bible for us, to lead us in worship, to punish us! We are not *members*, Mariche, we are commodities. (Again, a translator's note about the word "commodities": similar situation to above.)

Salome continues: When our men have used us up so that we look sixty when we're thirty and our wombs have literally dropped out of our bodies onto our spotless kitchen floors, finished, they turn to our daughters. And if they could sell us all at auction afterwards they would.

Agata and Greta exchange glances. Greta closes her eyes, one hand on her cheek, arthritic knuckles bulging like the rings of a Tudor king.

But, says Agata, Mariche raises a good point. Shouldn't we, even as the women of Molotschna, be acting in solidarity towards the freedom of our falsely accused men, if they are falsely accused.

Salome growls.

Ona quickly interjects, saying that this raises another question. It is possible, she says, the men in prison are not guilty of the attacks. But are they guilty of not *stopping* the attacks? Are they guilty of knowing about the attacks and doing nothing?

How should we know what they're guilty of or not? says Mariche.

But we do know, says Ona. We do know that the conditions of Molotschna have been created by man, that these attacks have been made possible, even the conception of these acts, the planning of these attacks, the rationale for these attacks within the minds of the men, because of the circumstances of Molotschna. And those circumstances have been created and ordained by the men, by the elders and by Peters.

Agata nods. Yes, she says, we know that.

(Autje and Neitje exchange glances. I surmise that this idea is new to them but they are prepared to accept it as fact if it means moving on, if it means less talk and more action.)

Agata adds: But we still have the question of time. We have very little left. There are certain aspects to our leaving that we can't resolve given our time constraints. We will have to put them aside for the time being and return to them at a later date. The guilt or innocence of the men in prison can't be known now, or perhaps ever, and nor can the guilt or innocence of the men in prison be the thing we hang our decision on, in terms of leaving. We've established our three reasons for leaving on the basis of love and of peace and of the nurturing of our souls, given to us by God, and the guilt or innocence of the men in prison has no direct co-relation to those reasons. Can we agree on that?

The women are pensive. Some nod with certainty (Salome and Mejal and Autje) but others are perhaps lost in thought, doubt and questions. (For clarity I will state: All the men in prison are known by, and related to, the women.)

Well? asks Agata. Half of us agree. And you others? This is a democracy, after all.

A what? asks Autje.

Three more women nod their assent: yes, their reasons for leaving are not contingent on the guilt or innocence of the men in prison. Only Mariche is left to answer.

Well, says Salome, that's seven out of eight, that's enough, this subject is closed.

But wait, says Mariche, aren't you suggesting that the attackers are as much victims as the victims of the attacks? That all of us, men and women, are victims of the *circumstances* from which Molotschna has been created?

Agata is quiet for a long moment. Then she says, In a sense, yes.

So then, says Mariche, even if the court finds them guilty or innocent, they are, after all, innocent?

Yes, says Ona, I would say so. Peters said these men are evil, the perpetrators, but that's not true. It's the quest for power, on the part of Peters and the elders and on the part of the founders of Molotschna, that is responsible for these attacks, because in their quest for power, they needed to have those they'd have power *over*, and those people are us. And they have taught this lesson of power to the boys and men of Molotschna, and the boys and men of Molotschna have been excellent students. In that regard.

But, says Mejal, don't we all want some type of power? She is lighting match after match because they continue to go out just as she brings them to the end of her cigarette. She is patient.

Yes, says Ona, I *think* so. But I'm not sure.

Oh, says Mariche sarcastically, power is another thing you don't believe in? Along with authority and love?

I never said I don't believe in love, explains Ona. Only that I am not sure what it means, exactly. In any case, what I said earlier was that I don't believe in the security that you say love brings.

You'll never know security, responds Mariche. Because of your Narfa.

That's true, says Ona. She seems calm, thoughtful. It's liberating, in a way, she adds.

Agata is, again, impatient. Ona, she says, love is another subject for another time.

And security? says Ona.

Greta interrupts: Isn't it always the subject?

Isn't what always the subject? asks Agata.

Love, says Greta.

How can something that is *always* the subject, and is eternal, also be one that is unknowable—at least according to Ona? says Mariche.

(At this, although it is an aside to note, I'm reminded of Montaigne's statement: "Nothing is so firmly believed as that which a man knoweth least." An embroidered image of these words was framed and hung in the dining hall in prison for a period of time. I do not know why.)

Mejal has managed to light her cigarette. Well, that's what makes it eternal, Mariche, she says. On and on and on. She exhales a little smoke between each "on." When we know something we stop thinking about it, don't we?

That's ridiculous, Salome says. Knowledge is fluid, it changes, facts change, become un-facts.

Neitje and Autje laugh at this, perhaps out of nervousness or exhaustion. Then they quickly apologize.

But seriously, says Salome. Are you telling me that you will stop thinking about something when you feel you "know" it? Are you out of your mind?

Mejal exhales again. She calmly tells Salome to fuck herself.

Order! Greta calls.

Salome ignores Greta. She launches into a tirade, saying that she doesn't even believe in eternity, nothing is eternal. In fact, she says, I no longer believe I will live forever. Her tone is defiant, a challenge, but the women do not take the bait.

(A note for context: Several years ago, a rumour spread from Chortiza. A substitute bishop had been brought to preach at the Chortiza church while the regular bishop lay dying at his home, and before the elders were able to elect a new bishop from their own colony. This substitute bishop came from a place in North America, and he had a wife who did not braid her hair. He allegedly told the congregation that he did not believe in the literal existence of heaven and hell. Certain members of the congregation were incredulous and alarmed and ran him off the colony. But not before this substitute bishop challenged them. He told them that not only did he not believe in the existence of heaven and hell, he firmly believed that neither did the members of the congregation, not really. He asked for a show of hands from the congregation: Who here today is the parent of an unsaved child, a rebellious child who has left the colony or who has claimed not to be a believer? Several hands were raised. The substitute bishop then directed his next question to these individuals who had raised their hands. If you love your children and you believe they are literally going to burn in the flames of hell for all eternity when they die, how can you sit here in this room calmly? How can you go to your home and enjoy a nice lunch of *vreninkje* and *platz* prepared by your wife and then settle into your warm bed with your feather comforter for a relaxing *maddachschlop*—afternoon nap— knowing that your child will soon be burning forever, screaming in agony, eternal pain? If you truly believed this, wouldn't you be doing everything in your power to get them to repent, to accept Jesus Christ into their hearts, to be forgiven? Wouldn't you be scouring the earth trying to find these wayward children, the ones who have left the colony, or who have been forced to leave the colony, the ones roaming the proverbial desert, the ones you deem to be sinners, but are still your children, your flesh and blood, your precious babies?

This substitute bishop was finally silenced and forced to leave the colony. The congregation agreed that having no church at all was better than this blasphemous garbage. But ever since, this idea of the nonexistence of heaven and hell has taken hold in some of the Mennonites, not only in Chortiza but in Molotschna as well, and is often used as a catalyst for provocation.

I wonder what Peters thinks about it. About precious babies, about eternity. And prodigal fathers.)

Well, says Agata calmly, if you don't believe in eternal life then we really must hurry now. You must agree that time is running out?

Ona says she would like to speak a little more on power.

The bishop and the elders of Molotschna have seized power over the ordinary men and women of Molotschna, she states. And the ordinary men have seized power over the ordinary women of Molotschna. And the ordinary women of Molotschna have seized power over . . . Ona pauses. The women are silent.

Nothing, says Ona, but our souls.

But that's blasphemy, says Mariche, if our souls are the manifestation of God, as you say. We can't have power over God. Also, she says, where does the desire for power come from? Is it not perfectly natural? Even the pigs in their filthy pen have established a pecking order.

But, says Ona, we're not pigs. Can't we be different? Do you believe that we evolved from animals or were created in the image of God?

Ona, says Agata gently. That's a fairly ridiculous question. You know the answer.

(A note: I am a little unsure myself what Agata thinks, although I assume she means the latter, that the women are created in God's image.)

Ona continues. One is probable, and certainly more conceivable, but the other is so beautiful, so hopeful, don't you think?

(Autje and Neitje glance at one another, as confused as I am at the moment. Their glance says, what is Ona saying now?)

I mean, says Ona, if we are created in God's image it allows *room* for our souls, for us to have them and to be in service to them. The power that we have is to give in to the power of our souls.

Mariche begins: I suppose if you've relinquished all practical considerations from your life and exist purely to satisfy your own crazy—

Now Salome interrupts. August, she says, what do *you* think? God's image or animals?

Animals? I ask. Do you mean as in—

Ona begins to laugh, rescuing me once again.

Salome elaborates. Yes! Do you think you were created in God's image, or that you evolved from animals?

Salome, says Ona. We can have souls either way.

I'm asking August, says Salome. Just answer the question.

No, says Agata. Not now. The one thing we can be sure of is that time exists, can't we? Because it's disappearing. And something that doesn't exist can't disappear. And without it, our goose is cooked.

But what about heaven? asks Neitje.

Her question is ignored because a person is climbing the ladder to the loft. It is Grant. He is "simple," as we say in Molotschna (although I am aware of the irony of this even as I write the word). He is reciting numbers, randomly, because he loves numbers, but hates having them arranged by others into recognizable equations. And he is "driving" his car. Cars are forbidden in Molotschna (not even rubber is allowed on the buggy wheels because rubber enables wheels to spin faster, allowing for a quicker escape into the world), but Grant is allowed to "drive" around the colony pretending to clutch a steering wheel with both hands, and to recite numbers in no discernible patterns.

We say hello to Grant. He tells us his father just won't die, he must stop eating bread made with white flour, he must be shot. (Death, in this case, is the reward, the compassionate choice. Grant is expressing his anxiety that his father was bedridden and in pain for so many years, and that he had wished to die, to join the Lord. He had asked to be shot but nobody would do it.) But Grant's father died years ago and Grant stays with Agata, or with other women in the colony when she gets weary of his endless talking, counting and singing. (He is one of the men who will accompany the women when/if they leave.)

Grant says, Six, nineteen, fourteen, one.

Alright Grant, says Agata. Those are fine numbers. Thank you. Would you like to sit quietly with us in the loft?

Grant offers to sing for us. He gets out of his car and sings a hymn relating to suffering followed by rest.

When he is finished we thank him, and he says we are most welcome. He gets back into his car and drives around the loft and honks his horn once or twice, then leaves, saying twelve, twelve, twelve . . .

Autje calls out, Thirteen!—and the other women shush her.

August Epp, At Night Between Meetings

THERE HAS BEEN AN INCIDENT. The women and children have left the loft. I am here alone, briefly finishing these notes for the day.

The young women, Autje and Neitje, left first, to check on the new calves. Then, while the remaining women were laughing at one thing or another, Autje and Neitje returned to the loft, followed by Klaas, Mariche's husband.

Autje called up as they ascended the ladder, Dad's home! She lent a cheerful inflection to her voice. She climbed slowly and Klaas was forced to fall in behind her on the ladder.

When they appeared, Autje and Neitje were visibly nervous and chagrined. Clearly they'd had no choice but to lead Klaas to the women.

Autje's announcement was a warning that allowed me just enough time to hide my papers and pens under the table. Ona tore the cheese wrapping with the writing, the pros and cons of the various options, from the wall and pushed those papers, too, under the plywood table.

When he appeared at last, Klaas demanded to know why the women had gathered in the hayloft.

Mariche tried to talk to him, to calm him. We were quilting, she said.

Klaas looked at me and laughed. Were they teaching you how to quilt, too? he asked. Finally, a useful skill for August to learn, considering what a dummkopf he is in the field.

The women laughed nervously along with him.

Yes, I said, playing along. I wanted to learn how to sew with thread so I could stitch up my students if they cut themselves accidentally at play.

Klaas repeated the word "students" and laughed again. He sniffed the air. He asked me if I didn't know better than not to smoke in a hayloft.

Mejal opened her mouth to speak. But before she could, I apologized loudly to Klaas. There will be no more smoking, I assured him.

August is learning how to quilt, he said, amused. He asked me if I was sure I knew what existed between my legs.

Oh, very, I said. (Smiling and tearing at my scalp.)

Hmm, said Klaas, I'm not so sure. Perhaps we should have a look.

Klaas, please stop talking that way in front of Julius and Miep, Mariche said, and his mood changed quickly.

Klaas became angry, wondering why his wife was here, why Nettie (Melvin) Gerbrandt was taking care of the other children and where his *faspa* was. He looked only at me when he spoke. He told me—because I am a man, a half-man, and deemed, barely, able to receive this type of business news—that he and Anton and Jacobo had returned from the city to get more animals to sell for bail money.

The judge is waiting, he said. Who has the key to the co-op?

I don't know, I said. (But I *do* know who has the key to the co-op. It's hanging in the tack room of Isaac Loewen, the caretaker of the co-op, and I silently asked God to forgive me. Or, if not, then to smote me on the spot.)

Where are the yearlings? asked Klaas. Why are they not in their barn?

I don't know, I said. (Again, I do know. Autje and Neitje released the yearlings into the field and they are down by the Sorghum Creek, grazing. Once again, I beg to be forgiven, or killed. Can I assume that since I now appear to be alive, I've been forgiven?)

Autje and Neitje stood behind Klaas, indicating with hand gestures to the other women that they had turned the yearlings out to graze.

Greta, Klaas's mother-in-law, chimed in. Many of the horses were sick, she told Klaas, and the vet from Chortiza had come by while Klaas was in the city and recommended the horses be quarantined for a period of two weeks so as not to spread the infection.

Klaas ignored her. Peters has instructed me to bring at least twelve horses to auction, he told me.

Yes, said Greta, but you'll get nothing for sick horses. You'll be fined for bringing sick horses to the auction.

Find the yearlings, he told the younger women, they're too young to be sick. Find them and tie them up.

Autje and Neitje once again descended the ladder.

I saw your team in the yard here at Earnest Thiessen's farm, said Klaas. They looked healthy, their eyes were clear and their coats shone.

Greta nodded. Yes, she said, because they are of an age that prevented them from contracting the illness affecting the other horses.

Klaas said, Bah, oba. He dismissed the explanation of age even though he had just mentioned that the yearlings were not old enough to be sick. He spat. Then he addressed Greta directly. Why were the women in Earnest Thiessen's loft?

Greta said: We needed to check on Earnest, to bring him food. We decided to do our quilting here in the loft because that way we can check on him regularly. We knew he wouldn't mind and we needed the extra room.

Is Earnest too senile to know that a gaggle of gossips are quilting in his loft? Klaas asked.

Greta nodded.

Where is the quilt then? asked Klaas.

We have just finished it, said Agata. It's been picked up by the Koop brothers to bring to the co-op.

I don't see evidence of the quilting table in the loft, or any odds and ends of fabric, said Klaas evenly. Nor have I seen the Koop brothers or the Koop brothers' team on the road between Molotschna and the co-op.

We have already cleaned up and were about to go home to make *faspa*, explained Agata. Aren't you hungry?

Greta spoke up to say the Koop brothers had mentioned they'd be taking an alternative route, through fallow fields.

And the real quilting room is being used for preserving, said Ona. It's chokecherry season. The jam will be delicious on fresh zwieback.

Klaas will not look at Ona or acknowledge anything she says. Ona is a ghost to him, or less, because of her Narfa, her spinsterdom, and her burgeoning belly. I have observed that being a ghost suits Ona.

When I passed the co-op it was locked, said Klaas, and there was nobody there.

Then the Koop brothers haven't got there yet, said Salome.

Do the Koop brothers have the key? asked Klaas.

How should I know? said Salome.

I need the key to get into the co-op to bring the money from the safe to Peters in the city.

Salome said, Well then, Peters should have told you where the key was.

Be quiet, said Klaas sharply.

He looked at me. Neitje told me the women were attending to a birth in Chortiza, he said.

We were, said Salome. There were difficulties. We'll have to go back.

Klaas maintained his gaze on me. Your responsibilities are here in Molotschna, he informed Salome.

I'm well aware of what my responsibilities are, said Salome.

I'm not talking to you. Be quiet, Klaas said again.

But you have been talking to me. You have just told me what my responsibilities are, haven't you?

Klaas turned his attention again to Greta. And your team, he said, I'm taking them.

Ruth and Cheryl? said Greta. No, you can't!

Klaas said he had no choice but to take Ruth and

Cheryl. He told the women they should go do the milking now and then to their homes and children and prepare food.

But they're old, said Greta. What will I do without my team?

You'll stay at home, Klaas responded.

He told Julius to leave the loft with him and return to their home. And he told Mariche to collect their other children from Nettie/Melvin. (Klaas and Mariche have many children, although I'm not sure exactly how many. They all have white hair bleached by the sun so that when they are darting about in their yard at dusk they look like fireflies or like the white seed heads of dandelions that float on the wind.)

Salome was the last to leave the loft. She spent some time lingering with Miep, admiring Miep's empire built from manure, while the other women descended the ladder, down from the loft to their earthly concerns.

Ona had to help Agata place her feet on the rungs because the feeling had gone out of them, a side effect of her edema. As Ona did this, Agata laughed and kissed the top of Ona's head. Breathe and slow down, Ona said. She reminded Agata of her habit of holding her breath while exerting herself, and then moving very quickly, too quickly, until the activity was complete and she could exhale once again.

Agata laughed again.

Don't laugh while you're on the ladder, Ona cautioned. Concentrate. (I wanted to tell Ona that Agata's breathing pattern while exerting herself reminded me of a balloon, pinched at the end to prevent the air from escaping, then released so that the air escapes quickly and noisily. But these women have never seen balloons. Perhaps they've seen the inflated pig bladders the children of Molotschna use as balls when Peters is away from the colony and they feel free to play. The moment passed.)

Agata at last managed to climb down the ladder and I heard her call out to the women that they would have to get an early start on the next quilt in the morning, immediately after milking.

I also heard Mariche asking Klaas why he'd given Julius so many cherries, so many that now his stomach hurt. Klaas laughed. Then he called up to Salome, telling her to hurry.

Salome yelled back down, Oh, you're talking to me? Her movements slow, glacial.

I offered to help Salome carry Miep down the ladder, but she refused. This was when we were alone briefly in the loft. I took advantage of the moment to tell her that the key to the co-op was in Isaac Loewen's tack room, on a nail above a blue salt block.

Forgive me for lying, I said.

She frowned.

I asked her if she knew how to navigate by the stars, if she knew where to find the Southern Cross.

She smiled and shook her head.

It is the supper hour now, I told her. While the men and women of the colony are in their homes, I will take the key and go to the co-op and get the safe. I don't know the code to open it, but I will take the entire safe and hide it. I told her the women could take it when they left Molotschna, if they left Molotschna, and find somebody to help them open it in a different place, another place.

Or perhaps, I said, Benjamin would give me a stick of dynamite, one that he uses to scare up the alligators in Sorghum Creek. You could use it to detonate the safe.

Wouldn't it be easier, whispered Salome, to find out the code?

I pleaded with her not to try to do that. And I asked her to forgive me once again, and then to go immediately to her duties so as not to arouse suspicion.

That was when Salome said my name.

August, she said, that money is ours anyway. There is nothing to forgive.

She carried Miep down the ladder and left the barn quickly.

I met Ona later, on the dirt path near my shed. The moon was bright.

I had gone out to pick some chokecherries for a night snack, because Ona had mentioned earlier that it was chokecherry season, and I had dribbled cherry juice down the front of my shirt. I returned to my shed, changed my clothing, then took my soiled shirt and walked to the wash house to leave it in the overnight bin. As I was leaving the wash house, I heard a woman say my name. Again. Two different women in one day saying my name. What a cacophony of emotions this aroused in me.

This second time, it was Ona. She was sitting on the low roof of the wash house, looking at the stars.

August! she said.

I looked up.

Come sit here with me.

I climbed a water barrel. And I sat beside her, in the night. The two of us. My knees shook.

She asked me why I was at the wash house and I told her. Then we were quiet.

Finally, I asked Ona if *she* knew of the Southern Cross. I pointed to the constellation of bright stars.

Of course, she said. She laughed.

I told her she and the women could use the Southern Cross, often referred to as the Crux, for navigation.

If you clench your right fist like this, I said. I took her hand and shaped it into a fist. I held it up against the stars. Her arm was rigid, her fist clenched, like a freedom fighter.

Now align your first knuckle with the axis of the Cross, I told her. I held her hand, her wrist. I felt God's majesty, overwhelming gratitude. My stomach flipped. My prayer had been answered.

Now, I said, the tip of your thumb, here, will indicate south.

Ona smiled, nodded, clapping her hands.

Will you show the others? I asked her.

Of course! she said again. We will have a lesson in navigation.

Ona, I said.

She looked at me, still smiling.

Did you already know about this little trick?

She laughed, nodded, said of course she did.

I smiled, too, sheepishly. I told her I wished there was something I could tell her that she didn't already know.

There is, she said. Tell me why you went to jail.

I stole a horse, I said.

Ona nodded solemnly, as though she had suspected this.

Then I explained everything to her. In London, after my father disappeared and my mother died, I had no place to live. I was in university, taking history classes, and had a nervous breakdown. I quit my studies (the Enlightenment) and I joined a group of anarchists and artists and musicians who were squatting on derelict land near the Gargoyle Wharf, in Wandsworth, next to the Thames. (This is where I learned to love ducks, though not to keep that ridiculous fact about myself to myself—especially in jail.)

Talking about semi-aquatic birds in jail, even the smallest detail, can trigger a severe beating, I told Ona, and she agreed I should have kept it to myself.

But when one loves something deeply it's very difficult to keep it a secret, isn't it? she said.

I mumbled, Yes. I glanced at her, then at the Southern Cross, then at my knees.

It was wonderful there, in Wandsworth, I continued. We lived simply, collectively. I built several buildings from material we took from old houses the city had torn down to make a freeway. We had concerts in our Eco Village, we had gardens, we strove to get along. There were hundreds of us, and one day we all went to Hyde Park to protest a bill that had been passed. It was a Criminal Justice bill that allowed the state to impose greater penalties for "antisocial" behaviours, such as ours. It outlawed raves and gatherings and even certain types of music that were "characterized by the emission of a succession of repetitive beats." I made imaginary quotation marks in the air as I told Ona this. I used what I thought was an authoritative voice. I spoke with a British accent.

Ona laughed. What is that music? she asked.

Techno, I said. Do you know what techno is?

No.

It is electronic dance music.

But you stole a horse? she said.

Yes, at the protest in Hyde Park. It was a horse being ridden by a police officer. The police officer had forced his horse to charge the protesters. I told Ona that some others at the protests—there were over fifty thousand people there, we heard later—had pulled the cop off the horse and the horse then stood, riderless, panicking, stomping its feet, rearing up against the crowd. I leapt onto the horse and rode away, around the crowd, out behind the people and the other police officers to a pond with a fountain where the horse could drink some water and cool off. I talked with the horse in what I hoped was a soothing voice. Nobody paid any attention to me or the horse. Eventually, I rode the horse all the way back to Wandsworth and kept him there, as a friend. A friend to all of us.

In fact, I said, I named him Frint. ("Friend" in Plautdietsch.)

Frint also did some work for us, because every being was expected to help. He carried wood sometimes, and other materials. He was exceptionally well-trained and fit.

Ona sat on the roof of the wash house and chuckled in the darkness. But you were caught? she asked.

Yes, I said. Eventually I was arrested for stealing Frint. It's a serious crime, to steal from a police officer.

And you went to jail, she said. Where it's a serious crime to admit that you love ducks.

Yes, I said. To Wandsworth Prison.

And was it difficult to be in jail? asked Ona.

Yes, I said. I had no visitors. The other squatters, my friends, were driven off their land and they moved on, away, and I never saw Frint again either.

Were you beaten? asked Ona.

Daily, I said.

Did you lose your faith? asked Ona.

Many times, I said. I wanted to kill several of my cell-mates. And most of the guards.

Were you afraid? asked Ona.

Always, I said. Always.

Minutes of the Women Talking

IT IS VERY EARLY, and still dark. I haven't slept since talking with Ona on the roof. I have lit a kerosene lamp so I can see what I'm writing.

The milking is done, and all of the women, except for Mariche and Autje, are in the loft. Greta is pacing, and periodically going to the window to peer into the dark. Her balance is not good. She has fallen several times in the last few months and has broken some ribs and her collarbone. Mejal asks her to concentrate on lifting her feet higher when she takes steps, not to shuffle, in order to avoid tripping, but Greta is very tired and her body is heavy and it is apparent that every piece of it hurts.

Agata has put her feet into Ona's lap and Ona is rubbing them, trying to regain the circulation of blood. Ona sings quietly, "On the Old Rugged Cross," and Agata sings every two or three words with her, although she is fighting for breath. Salome (Miep is not here, nor Salome's other children) is absentmindedly braiding Neitje's hair, tugging so tightly that Neitje must beg for mercy.

You are blinding me, she tells her mother/aunt.

Salome repeats her question to Neitje: Did you tell the others about our meeting?

Neitje confirms that she did.

Salome murmurs in approval and asks how the women reacted to Neitje's news.

Most of the women agreed to meet at the yearling barn this evening after *faspa*, Neitje says.

And what about the other women? asks Salome.

The other women didn't say anything, says Neitje. Some didn't want to hear it. Some walked away. Bettina Kreuger batted the air at imaginary pests.

Mejal interrupts. Don't worry, she tells Salome. The menfolk of the Do Nothing women are still in the city with Peters, and their women won't be able to inform them of the plan.

What if Klaas found out? asks Salome. Where is Mariche, anyway?

Klaas won't remember anything he was told, even if he was told, says Agata.

Mejal asks Salome if Miep is with Nettie/Melvin.

She is, says Salome. But she's not well today and the pills are not helping her. I suspect the pills are for animals, not people.

But Miep is small, says Mejal. They'll work.

Miep is small, Salome says. But she's not a calf.

Would you like to hear about the dream I had last night? Ona asks Agata.

Agata is resting her head in her hand. She says: In all honesty, Ona, no, I don't.

Ona smiles.

But later, yes, says Agata. She returns Ona's smile.

August, says Ona. Did you dream last night?

Yes, I say.

In fact, I didn't dream because I didn't sleep—unless my conversation with Ona on the wash house roof was a dream? Ona continues to sing. Then she stops. Mom, she says, I dreamt that you had died, and in my dream I said, But if you are dead then there is nobody to catch me if I fall. And then in my dream you came back from death, you were tired, your feet hurt, but you were happy to come back one last time, and you said: Then don't fall.

The other women laugh.

I long to tell Ona that I would catch her if she fell.

Agata pats Ona's hand. Ona, she says, we are born and then we live and then we die, and then we don't live again except in heaven. Where there will be justice.

And respect, says Greta. Her arms shoot up suddenly like an American football referee indicating a touchdown has been scored.

Well then, says Ona, we were in heaven together. In my dream.

But Ona, says Mejal, if you were in heaven you would have many people to catch you if you fell. But you'd be in heaven, so you wouldn't fall.

Salome says: You might trip, though. You're clumsy. (I can see that Salome is exasperated with this subject.)

Unless heaven is part of a dream, says Ona. Or unless dreams are illogical.

Well, that they are, says Agata.

I don't know, says Ona, perhaps they are the most logical experience we can ever have.

Heaven is real, says Mejal. Dreams are not real.

How do you know? asks Ona. And don't we dream of heaven? Isn't heaven entirely a dreamt thing? Although that doesn't make it unreal.

Agata firmly changes the subject. Where is Mariche? she asks. And Autje. Look at the sky, she adds, pointing to the light on the horizon.

Mejal places small remnants of fabric and spools of thread around the table to make it appear as though the women are preparing to quilt.

In case Klaas comes back, she explains. When she finishes, she turns to Salome and tells her in a soft, worried voice that she has stopped bleeding.

Salome curses, then makes a joke about who the father might be.

Mejal lifts her ochre finger (secret life!) to silence Salome.

(I observe that each time Salome is upset or angered she yanks on Neitje's braid, and now Neitje has endured enough. She pulls away from Salome and gives the task of braiding her hair to her grandmother, Agata.)

Mejal tells Salome that Andreas, her husband, is frightened each month when Mejal bleeds yet doesn't die. It confuses him. She laughs.

That's a ridiculous exaggeration, says Greta. Of course Andreas understands the female cycle. (It's clear she disapproves of Mejal's lack of respect for her husband.)

Have you not explained it to Andreas? asks Salome.

Mejal laughs again. It's funnier that he's startled by it, she says.

You mean because you don't die when you bleed? asks Ona. Does he think you're a witch?

At last, Mariche has appeared and is climbing the ladder to the loft. Autje is behind her, helping.

Greta rushes to Mariche, takes her in her arms.

Ona and Agata look away.

Salome stands up. What has happened? she asks. What has happened?

Mariche's face is bruised and cut. Her arm is in a sling fashioned from a feed bag. Autje also has a bruise on her cheek in the shape of four fingers and a thumb. The two take their places at the table.

Greta asks: Is he gone?

Mariche, ever defiant, answers: Would I be here now if he wasn't?

Neitje, her hair finally in a braid, goes to sit beside her pal Autje. She says nothing, has nothing to tell her or to give her, but synchronizes her breathing with Autje's. They look ahead, towards something I can't identify, not empty space. And they are silent.

Then let's begin, says Agata. Yesterday was a day for talking, today is one for action. Tomorrow the men will return. Is it accurate to say that we have all, more or less, decided to leave before that happens? That we have overruled the other options of staying and fighting, because we are pacifists, and because—

Salome interrupts: Or because we wouldn't win.

No, says her mother, we have ruled out staying and fighting because our faith consists of core values, one of them being pacifism, and we have no homeland but our faith, and we are servants to our faith, and by being such we are assured eternal peace in heaven.

Salome nearly spits, Well that peace sure as fuck is not happening in Molotschna.

Salome, please do not curse, says Agata. She suggests that Salome do twelve jumping jacks instead.

Neitje laughs.

Will doing twelve jumping jacks bring peace to Molotschna? asks Salome.

Mariche, with her ravaged face, says: I thought today was a day of action, not talk.

The other women laugh softly, indulging her this morning, acknowledging her brave humour.

Yes, continues Agata, we have ruled out the option of doing nothing because by doing nothing we are not protecting our children, who were given to us by God to protect and nurture—

Mariche interrupts: But how can we be sure they won't be harmed when we leave Molotschna?

We *can't* be sure, says Ona. But we can be sure they *will* be harmed if we stay. Ona and Mariche lock eyes.

Can't we? asks Ona.

Mariche is silent. Her eyes are wet. She is folding a piece of fabric into a smaller piece, pulling at the threads.

The other women look away, towards the light coming up over the horizon and through the window into Ernie Thiessen's hayloft.

I blow out my kerosene lamp. The light in the loft now is adequate and the women are vulnerable today, solemn, wounded, anxious. As well, I sense that Mariche wishes to remain in the shadows, uninterrogated. The sounds of animals are loud outside, and wind from the open window lifts the strands of hair that have escaped Ona's forbidden loose bun.

How many times will we pack our bags and disappear into the night? asks Greta.

Autje and Neitje exchange glances. (They are literalists and I know they are likely thinking: We've *never* done that, have we?)

Greta, what are you referring to? Agata asks.

This is no time for a history lesson, says Mariche. As I understand it, what we women have determined is that we want, and believe we are entitled to, three things.

What are they? asks Greta.

Mariche says: We want our children to be safe. She has begun to cry softly and is finding it difficult to speak, but she continues. We want to be steadfast in our faith. We want to think.

Agata claps her hands once, holds them together in midair and says, Praise God. Greta, like a football official once again, raises her arms above her head.

The old women are jubilant. Salome and Mejal smile.

Salome says, Yes, that's it.

Precisely, says Mejal.

Well, it's not quite *precisely* put, Salome says. But it sounds perfect to me. A perfect beginning.

Salome, will you use your last breath on earth to correct me? Mejal asks.

Yes, if that's what is needed, says Salome.

Ona's eyes have become big. She appears to be in a reverie, or enraptured. This is the beginning of a new era, she says. This is our manifesto. (She says "manifesto" in English but with her Mennonite inflection it sounds like "mennofasto.")

What is that? asks Autje.

Please direct all of your queries to Salome, says Mejal. She is willing to use her last breath on earth to educate her stupid friends.

Salome laughs. She objects: I didn't say you were stupid, Mejal. Only that you used the word "precisely" imprecisely.

Mejal rolls a smoke and suggests she should be tortured to death for the infraction.

What's a manifesto? asks Autje again.

The other women frown. They look at Ona, who smiles. I'm not entirely sure, she says, but I believe it is a statement of some kind. A guide.

Then Ona looks at me and asks, Well?

Yes, I agree, it's a statement. A statement of intent. Sometimes revolutionary.

Agata and Greta exchange alarmed glances.

No, no, August, says Agata, it cannot be revolutionary. We are not revolutionaries. We are simple women. We are mothers. Grandmothers.

Revolutionaries are soldiers, adds Greta, often armed with assault rifles or bombs or some such thing. That is the opposite of what we are. (Within the Molotschna Colony any reference to revolution invokes the Russian

Revolution, which is not seen to have been a good thing for the Mennonites.)

But are we willing to die for our cause? asks Ona.

Neitje and Autje shake their heads.

Yes, says Salome, of course.

Neitje and Autje exchange alarmed glances touchingly similar to the glances exchanged by their grandmothers just a moment ago.

Are you willing to *kill* for our cause? asks Ona.

No, says Salome.

But you'll allow yourself to *be* killed for our cause? asks Ona.

Well, no, says Salome, ideally not.

Because you don't want to make a murderer out of somebody else? asks Ona. Or because you value your individual life over the cause?

I don't know, says Salome impatiently. And time is passing.

Ona is only trying to get a precise read, Mejal says. Isn't precision your specialty? The subject of your last breath on earth?

Listen, says Agata. That's enough.

I have now raised my hand, with trepidation, and Agata says, Yes, August?

I have asked, once again, to be forgiven for using words recklessly and inciting unnecessary debate.

Ona vomits into the feed pail next to her. She apologizes. Then she looks at me. I like the word "revolutionary," she says. There are flecks of vomit on her chin.

Salome picks up a piece of straw and wipes Ona's chin. She whispers something to Ona, fiercely.

Ona nods. She looks towards the window. She nods again. (A small revolution within a larger one?)

Let's move on, says Agata. Can we agree that we want only to protect our children, keep our faith, and think? That we are not revolutionaries (or animals)? And that the question of whether we would die for our cause is not something we need to ask at this point since we have more urgent matters to tend to?

Yes, says Mejal. But I have one further question I'd like to raise. It has to do with the Biblical exhortation that women obey and submit to their husbands. How, if we are to remain good wives, she says, can we leave our men? Is it not disobedient to do so?

Our first and more pressing duty, says Salome, is to our children, to their safety.

But not biblically speaking, says Mejal.

We can't read, says Salome, so how are we to know what is in the Bible?

You are being difficult, says Mejal. We have been told what is in the Bible.

Yes, says Salome, by Peters and the elders and by our husbands.

Right, says Mejal. And by our sons.

Our sons! says Salome. And what is the common denominator linking Peters and the elders and our sons and husbands?

I am sure you will inform us, says Mejal.

They are all men! says Salome.

Of course, says Mejal, I know that much. But who else would interpret the Bible for us?

My point, says Salome, is that by leaving, we are not necessarily disobeying the men according to *the Bible*, because we, the women, do not know exactly what is in the Bible, being unable to read it. Furthermore, the only reason why we feel we need to submit to our husbands is because our husbands have told us that the Bible decrees it.

If your husband, she asks Mejal, told you that God, in the Bible, through the words of the various male prophets and disciples, or through the words of Jesus Himself, had made it clear that he, your husband, should punch you hard in the face when you question his motives—and also that he should lash his small children with a horse whip when they left the barn door open accidentally, and that you must do the same—would you agree with him?

Mejal rolls her eyes—and also, a cigarette.

Would you assume that he knew this to be God's law? Salome insists.

Ona quotes from Ecclesiastes: *A time for love and a time for hate. A time for war and a time for peace.*

Agata raises her eyebrows. Why are you bothering to get involved in this discussion? she asks.

The Bible suggests there is a time for hate and a time for war, says Ona. Do we believe in that?

The women are silent.

No, says Agata, we don't.

We hate war, says Neitje.

Autje laughs.

Agata smiles, acknowledging the girls. She moves her upper body to the left, to the right, to the left, a subtle dance she performs when she appreciates a joke, indicating she gets it, it's a good one.

Mariche says, It's probably safe to say that there are some gaps in our understanding of the Bible. We should move on. She lifts her chin to the window, to the sun, a quick gesture.

I agree there are gaps, Salome says. But the problem is more specific than mere gaps.

Chasms? asks Neitje. Autje smirks.

The issue, continues Salome, pointedly ignoring Neitje, is the male interpretation of the Bible and how that is "handed down" to us.

Ona states simply: Yes, our inability to read or write puts us at a great disadvantage in any negotiation over the interpretation of the Bible.

Agata slaps her hand on the plywood. This is interesting, she says, but Mariche is right. We're running out of time. Can we agree that we will not feel guilt—

But how can we control our feelings? interrupts Mariche.

Agata continues: —about disobeying our husbands by leaving Molotschna because we are not entirely convinced that we are being disobedient? Or that such a thing as disobedience even exists?

Oh, it exists, says Mariche.

Yes, says Salome, as a word, as a concept and as an action. But it isn't the correct word to define our leaving Molotschna.

It might be *one* word, says Mariche, to define our leaving.

True, says Salome, one word out of many. But it's a word that the men of Molotschna would use, not God.

That's true, says Mejal. God might define it otherwise, our leaving.

And how do you think God would define our leaving? asks Ona.

As a time for love, a time for peace, says Mejal.

Aha! says Ona. She claps her hands joyfully.

Salome smiles.

Mejal is radiant. Agata moves her upper body to the left, then to the right.

(I am struck by a thought: Perhaps it is the first time the women of Molotschna have interpreted the word of God for themselves.)

We will feel anguish and we will feel sorrow and we will feel uncertainty and we will feel sadness, but not guilt, says Agata.

Mariche amends: We may *feel* guilty but we will know we are not guilty.

The other women nod, eagerly. Mejal says, We may *feel* homicidal but we know we are not killers.

Ona says, We may *feel* vengeful but we will know we are not raccoons.

Salome is laughing. We may feel lost, she says, but we will know we are not losers.

Speak for yourself, says Mejal.

I always do, says Salome. You should try it too.

Mejal impersonates Salome, echoing her words in an imperious, frog-like voice.

One last thing before we move on, says Greta. There is the question of re-educating our boys and men. Isn't that also something we'd like?

Not *like*, says Salome, not entirely. (At this correction from Salome, the young women again mime killing themselves.) Re-educating our boys and men is something we're *obligated* to do if we are to uphold the tenet of pacifism and non-conflict that is central to our faith and must be adhered to if we are to know eternal peace in heaven!

Yes, says Greta (with epic weariness).

And if we are to protect our children, says Ona.

Yes, that too, says Greta. And adds, So shouldn't it be a part of our plan?

The manifesto, says Neitje, and Autje giggles.

Yes, says Greta. Part of the manifesto.

Both Neitje and Autje burst into laughter. It appears they find the word "manifesto" unbearably funny.

Salome says, We will be doing the work of re-education organically—(Oh for fuck's sake, *organically*, says Mejal)— while we raise our young male children to be compassionate and respectful.

Salome flicks a piece of rolled-up fabric at Mejal, who proceeds to burn a hole straight through its middle with her cigarette and then peers through the hole at Salome, with one dark eye.

Salome laughs. Put that in your quilt, she tells Mejal. It will add character.

You mean our imaginary quilt, says Mejal.

But what of the boys left behind? says Greta.

Salome turns suddenly solemn. She puts her hand up and asks for a clarification. Have we already determined the cutoff age for the boys who are allowed to join us? she asks.

The women are silent for a moment. Then Agata says she has been thinking about this and would like to make a proposal. The subject of our boys and men is a complex one, she says. We love our sons, and with some legitimate reservations we love our husbands, too, if only because we have been instructed to.

You're confusing love with obedience, says Mariche.

Perhaps in your case that is true, Mariche, but it is not necessarily true for the other women in the colony, Agata says. In any case, we must love, or show love, to all people. It is the preeminent word of God (as interpreted by men presumably) to love one another as God loves us, and to love our neighbour as we would hope that our neighbour loves us.

(I hear Salome inhaling at length.)

Autje and Neitje once again put their heads down on the table. Neitje has offered Autje a bite of a sausage she's been chewing on since the meeting began.

Autje frowns, closes her eyes.

Neitje places her hand gently on Autje's cheek, eclipsing the bruise left by Autje's father.

Agata presents her proposal: All boys under the age of fifteen must accompany the women.

Accompany us to where? asks Mariche.

Mariche, says Greta. You know we don't know exactly where we're going.

Mejal adds: How could we know? We've never left Molotschna and we don't have a map, and even if we did have a map we don't know how to read it.

Salome asks: How do you mean, *must*? We're forcing them to leave with us?

Agata continues, undeterred. Fifteen is the age of baptism and those boys who have been baptized into the church and are now fully fledged members are considered to be men, and so they are presently in the city with the older men. The boys under fifteen, and Cornelius, and Grant, are here on the colony. They are childlike because they require special care. Of course they must leave with us. Our duty and instinct, and our desire, as we've established, is to protect our children. Not only our daughters.

The women speak at once, and again I'm unable to decipher their individual voices.

Please, says Agata. One at a time.

What will we do if those boys don't want to leave, if they refuse to leave? Mariche wonders. We can't carry fourteen-year-old boys on our back.

That's true, says Agata. We can't force them to leave with us but we will explain everything that we've discussed here in the loft, why we think it would be best for them to leave with us. We will try to *influence* our sons.

Autje and Neitje have lifted their heads from the table.

Neitje says, The boys would be able to read the map.

If we had one, says Autje.

I raise my hand.

Autje smiles. Yes, Mr. Epp?

I tell the women that I'm still in the process of procuring the world map that I know to exist in Chortiza colony.

The women laugh. (I don't know why.)

Ona returns to her mother's words. For the women of Molotschna to agree to try to influence their sons is truly revolutionary, she says.

No, says Agata. It's instinctive. We are their mothers. They are our children. We have collectively and according to the tenets of our faith and to the definition, at least to our knowledge, of love and peace, and the criteria for eternal life in heaven, decided what is best for them, and we will follow through accordingly. Our animal instincts have joined forces with our intellects, which have lurked and languished in the shadows long enough, and with our souls, which are the manifestation of God. How is that revolutionary? (Agata is now very short of breath.)

Will the boys who refuse to leave with us be allowed to stay in the colony? Mariche asks.

Of course, says Agata, we'll entrust their care to the Do Nothing women and to their fathers, who are due to return soon—tomorrow, anyway.

Mejal says, But that would be very sad.

Yes! says Agata. It would be very sad. But sadness can't be avoided. And we'll endure it.

Salome, says Mariche. What will your Aaron do? Will he leave?

Salome ignores the question. Instead she asks Agata: Will we invite the men and the boys who stay behind to join us later when we've established a new community?

I'm not sure, says Agata. As we know, the young men
of Molotschna often marry at age sixteen and the boys
who stay behind will likely marry girls from Chortiza or
beyond, perhaps from Hiakjeke. (Translator's note: a
colony north of Chortiza that means, in our language,
"Here, look," supposedly the answer to the question,
Where are we?) They will likely not want to uproot
themselves after that.

But if they did want to join us, says Mejal, they'd be
able to?

Agata is silent. She blinks rapidly and looks towards
the rafters.

Perhaps, says Ona, they could join us if they sign our
manifesto and adhere to it.

Salome says she's afraid the manifesto would be altered
or gradually degraded by the men. They might sign only
to be allowed back with the women, but wouldn't follow
the terms afterwards.

Mejal agrees. And then we'd be back to where we
started, she says.

Listen, says Agata. We're embarking on a journey.
We're initiating a change that we have interpreted, over
the last two days, as being God's will and a testament to
our faith, and responsibilities and natural instincts as
mothers and as human beings with souls. We must
believe in it.

Greta elaborates: We don't know everything that
will happen. We'll have to wait and see. For now, we've
made our plan.

Ona turns to me. August, do you think the artist

Michelangelo knew what his painting would look like before he started?

I don't know, I say.

Mariche says, It's not likely.

Or a photograph, says Ona. Does the person taking the photograph know what it will look like while he is taking it?

In the case of the photograph, I say, the photographer might possibly have a better idea of what the work will look like than the artist, Michelangelo, would have of the final expression of his art.

Ona thanks me for this explanation. We, the women, are artists, she says.

Mariche scoffs. Artists of anxiety, she says.

Ona smiles at me. I smile at Ona.

Agata takes Ona's hand who takes Salome's hand who takes Mejal's hand who takes Neitje's hand who takes Autje's hand who takes Mariche's hand who takes Greta's hand who takes Agata's hand.

The women look at me.

Agata drops her hand from Greta's and takes my hand and I will put down my pen and take Greta's hand, trying not to put pressure on her swollen knuckles.

We have sung. Agata began, and we all joined in: the two older women with gusto, the two youngest with mortification, mumbling; the ones in between with resignation, although artfully.

We are in Earnest Thiessen's hayloft, between earth and sky, and this was perhaps the last time I would hear Ona sing. We sang "For the Beauty of the Earth."

> *For the beauty of the earth,*
> *For the beauty of the skies,*
> *For the Love which from our birth*
> *Over and around us lies:*
> *Christ, our God, to Thee we raise*
> *This our Sacrifice of Praise.*
> *For the beauty of each hour*
> *Of the day and of the night,*
> *Hill and vale, and tree and flower,*
> *Sun and moon and stars of light:*
> *Christ, our God, to Thee we raise*
> *This our Sacrifice of Praise.*
> *For the joy of ear and eye,*
> *For the heart and brain's delight,*
> *For the mystic harmony*
> *Linking sense to sound and sight:*
> *Christ, our God, to Thee we raise*
> *This our Sacrifice of Praise.*
> *For the joy of human love,*
> *Brother, sister, parent, child,*
> *Friends on earth, and friends above;*
> *For all gentle thoughts and mild:*
> *Christ, our God, to Thee we raise*
> *This our Sacrifice of Praise.*
> *For each perfect Gift of Thine*
> *To our race so freely given,*

Graces human and Divine,
Flowers of earth, and buds of Heaven:
Christ, our God, to Thee we raise
This our Sacrifice of Praise.

Greta has suggested we sing another hymn. She asks the women if they'd like to sing "Nearer, My God, to Thee."

I am emotional. I don't know what is wrong with me. Ona is looking at me. I raise my hand.

You can speak whenever you want to speak, August, says Agata, and you don't have to raise your hand. You're the teacher! She laughs.

The others stare at me.

Tears are rolling down my cheeks. I can hardly see the paper to write these words. I see Mariche purse her lips, look away. This half-man. Of dubious origin. Autje and Neitje appear to be as mortified by my crying as I am.

This is what I wonder: Did my mother once love Peters? Had he been different than he is now? Kind? Another sort of person, if only he were not trapped in the crucible of this crushing experiment? Is it a sin to hope that this is so? Would he understand my fear? Console me? I force the tears to stop by focusing on the definition of liminal space. I want to share this definition with Ona. But perhaps I won't, now, have that opportunity.

Instead I ask the women if I may share with them a fact regarding the hymn that Greta has suggested: "Nearer, My God, to Thee."

Salome frowns but says, Of course, August, but hurry, look. She points to the window, to the light, which has

suddenly become the central character in our story, the
fearsome catalyst.

"Nearer, My God, to Thee," I begin, is the song that
the passengers of the *Titanic* sang as the ship was sinking.

I look at Ona.

She says she doesn't know of this ship, but it is the song
she would sing as well if she were on a doomed vessel.

Mariche adds: And if there was nothing else to be
done.

Yes, says Ona, if there was nothing else to be done.

None of the women in the loft have heard of the
Titanic. None of the women in the loft have seen an
ocean. Their measured and polite attention to my fact is
embarrassing. They are silent, nodding, giving the fact
its due. Such torment in my heart, titanic. This fact was
meant for Ona. But how stupid of me to offer such a gift,
as though to imply that the women's plan is doomed.
How selfish of me.

Greta, mercifully, again suggests that we sing now.

We have finished singing "Nearer, My God, to Thee." I
wished so badly to hold Ona's hand while singing rather
than Agata's and Greta's. God, forgive me.

Now there is work to do.

Agata insists that we must stop talking through flowers
(a loose translation of the expression she has used in
Plautdietsch). The time is nigh for the women to prepare
for departure.

Most of the others nod. Mariche frowns but says nothing.

Things have happened overnight, says Agata, since our meeting ended yesterday.

She continues: I went to use the biffy after *faspa* and I heard a terrible moaning from across the northwest field, next to my house. Because of my edema (she pauses and takes a breath, allowing the other women to linger and luxuriate on the proper name for what is ailing her) I was keeping my feet up, resting them on Autje's old cradle, the light-blue one with the angels, the one that Kurt made before his spine cracked.

I wasn't able to get up to investigate, she continues, but the moaning was coming closer to my house, and closer still, then even closer, and I could also hear horses and the wheels of a buggy on the gravel, and eventually there was a knock at my door.

Ona encourages her mother to pick up the pace of the narrative by clearing her throat and nodding vigorously, her eyes wide.

Agata continues: It was Klaas.

Agata tells the women that Klaas was suffering from the pain of a rotten molar. (Agata has been the colony dentist since her father, the previous colony dentist, died and left his tools in her care.)

Mariche nods. Yes, she says, I knew that already. His breath has been putrid. She waves her hand beneath her nose, scowling.

Salome asks: But was this before or after he left the bruises on your face, Mariche?

Mariche swats the question away and motions, by flicking her bitten-off finger, to Agata to continue.

Agata explains that she agreed to pull Klaas's rotten tooth, but had to anesthetize him first. He agreed, and just before Agata clamped the ether-soaked rag on his face she asked him if he knew where the other two men were, the ones who had returned to Molotschna with him, Yasch (Anton) and Jacobo.

Klaas told her they were drunk on mistletoe vodka, lying out in some fallow field near the yearling barn.

I told Klaas he and the others drank too much, says Agata. He sulked. And he said that everybody talked about how much he drank but nobody ever talked about how thirsty he was.

Mariche snorts. I've heard that before.

Agata put Klaas under and went to work on the tooth. She removed it quickly, left Klaas unconscious, and then got into his buggy and rode his team to the summer kitchen where she loaded it up with cheese, sausage, bread, flour, salt, eggs and water.

Salome asks: Is the bread the bracka?

Agata confirms that it is.

(Translator's note: Bracka is the dried bread needed for long journeys. It is dipped or soaked in water, to soften it, and it lasts for a very long time. And a second note: Had Agata noticed Ona and me up on the wash house roof?)

Agata returned to her house, unloaded the supplies, hid them in her bedroom and waited for Klaas to wake up. As Klaas was preparing to leave he asked Agata why his horses were soaked in sweat.

Ona interrupts: Was he able to speak after just having his molar removed?

Yes, says Agata, he used hand gestures along with words.

Agata replied that he must have driven his team hard, as always (Greta mutters: Too hard), to her place, that the surgery had been quick, and that the horses hadn't had time to recover.

Salome interrupts: Well, now that he's had that tooth pulled he might be in a better mood.

Mariche cocks her head and glares at Salome.

I'm sorry, Salome says. But I am being genuine, hopeful.

Perhaps Salome's right, Greta says, soothing both women. He might be less combative without an aching tooth. Maybe Salome's right.

I don't mind Salome being right, says Mariche. I just don't like it when she *thinks* she's right.

There is a consensus amongst the women on this point. They nod at each other, chewing on the significant difference between being right and thinking one is right.

Autje breaks the silence. We—she gestures at her mother and herself—might never see my father again, she says.

The other women remain silent, brooding on this too.

All of us here in the loft are leaving family members behind, Agata reminds her gently. Husbands, brothers, fathers, sisters, aunts and uncles.

But not children, says Ona.

Some children, Salome corrects her.

Adult children, says Ona. She, like Salome, has several brothers in the city.

But not all adult children, says Agata.

That's right, says Greta.

Greta removes Mariche's kerchief and strokes her hair. Mariche leans into the tender embrace of her mother.

Let's talk about our sadness after we have nailed down our plan, suggests Agata.

The women's expressions are stern, grim, desolate and tight with tension, but they nod in agreement.

Agata reminds the women that she has secured a great amount of food for the trip, that they will pack it in her buggy later tonight. (Agata is a widow. Her husband, Kurt, died many years ago—from fright, according to Peters. In Peters' account, Kurt saw the devil in a clearing beyond the mile road west of the yearling barn when he was shooting crows, crows that had been destroying his corn, and dropped dead immediately.

In Agata's account—supported by Ona though not entirely by Salome or by Agata's sons, all grown men, married and in the city presently—Kurt put the .22 to the side of his head and blew his brains out. Ona's Narfa, the colonists say, had been latent, simmering but not unmanageable, until her father died. Afterwards, she committed her life to dreamy eccentricity, and also to facts, curiously, and to her seemingly preferred status as a pariah, as the devil's daughter, and God-given burden to the colony. I contend a lighter, less intrusive presence has never been known.)

Agata asks the women what other preparations were made last night.

The women speak at once. Greta can't help but laugh. She asks the others to be quiet so that Autje and Neitje can tell of their accomplishment.

Autje and Neitje are smiling, excited yet bashful, eager to share their news.

Autje begins to speak, then stops and moans. The bruise on her face makes it painful to talk.

Salome reaches across the table and pats her hand.

Ona says, Oh, Autje, *leibchen*, don't speak. Neitje will explain.

Here is a summary of Neitje's account: Last night, after Klaas went to get his rotten tooth pulled by Agata, Autje snuck out of the house and ran to get Neitje. (Neitje's father/uncle, Salome's husband, is in the city with the other men.) The two of them, Autje and Neitje, ran to Greta's barn and hurriedly, in complete darkness, saddled up Ruth and Cheryl and rode them to Chortiza colony. There they met up with the Koop brothers behind the Chortiza church, near an open pit used for burning animal carcasses, where the youth of both colonies spend leisure time together on Wednesday and Sunday evenings.

The girls managed to convince the Koop brothers to harbour Ruth and Cheryl overnight, in the brothers' barn. In the morning, early, after Klaas had left for the city (angrily, without Ruth and Cheryl, but grateful to have had his rotten tooth removed), the Koop brothers would return Ruth and Cheryl to Molotschna, to Greta's barn. Greta's beloved team would be safe and ready to leave with the women on their journey.

When Neitje finishes, most of the women are smiling, nodding and appreciative.

Salome, however, is frowning. How were you able to convince the Koop brothers to hide Ruth and Cheryl in their father's barn? she asks.

It was easy, says Neitje quickly, because the Koop brothers like us. She and Autje exchange glances.

And how did you girls get back to Molotschna if Ruth and Cheryl stayed behind in the Koop brothers' barn? asks Salome.

The Koop brothers brought us back, says Neitje, with a trace of defiance. We rode behind them on their horses, clutching their waists.

You were clutching their waists? asks Salome. Clutching their waists?

Neitje nods, and doesn't avert her gaze from Salome's.

What did you do for the Koop brothers, asks Salome, in return for them hiding Ruth and Cheryl?

The young women are silent.

Well? asks Salome.

Agata chastens Salome. It's none of our business, she says. What's done is done, Greta's beloved team is safe and the girls are none the worse for wear.

Salome persists. She is angry with Neitje—and with Autje, presumably. She raises her voice. Two old brood mares are not worth demeaning yourselves over, she says.

Neitje mutters something.

Please repeat that, says Salome. I can't hear you.

Neitje glares at her mother/aunt. She says, softly, You

have demeaned yourself many times for much less than
two good horses.

What are you talking about? Salome demands.

Neitje is silent.

Salome repeats her demand.

Neitje won't speak.

Salome, again, demands that Neitje speak.

Neitje shakes her head no.

Raising her voice now, Salome says that she has only
ever done what was required of her in order to keep the
peace, that Neitje has no business criticizing her behaviour
as a wife and mother, that her behaviour, her submission,
her own pain, has prevented Neitje's father from violating
Neitje herself, that—

Agata puts her hand up.

At last, Neitje speaks. Oh, she says to Salome, should
I thank you?

Agata says quietly: Salome, that's enough. There's no
time for this.

Salome's eyes are bayonets. She mutters obscenities,
jabs at the air, tugs at the front of her dress, the rectangu-
lar panel of fabric, de rigueur, that is worn to conceal her
breasts . . . Girls who aren't virgins can't get married, she
says. She is raging.

Ona pulls gently on Salome's sleeve, murmuring
words I can't make out. (She is telling Salome, I believe,
that the laws of Molotschna are not the same as the laws
of the world, that it doesn't matter if the girls are virgins
or not.)

What do you know of the world? Salome asks Ona.

Nothing, says Ona.

Ona has succeeded in calming Salome. Their faces are an inch apart, as though Ona is breathing sweetness, peace, into the mind of her angry sister.

Fair enough, Salome says. But tell me, Neitje, did you girls tell the Koop brothers of our plan to leave?

The young women shake their heads.

You're sure of that? says Salome.

The young women nod their heads. They are sure.

We are not idiots, says Neitje.

I am not so sure of that, replies Salome, her voice rising, allowing the Koop brothers to have their way with you for the safety of two near-death nags—

Agata interrupts. Salome, she says again, enough.

Salome is quiet, breathing heavily.

Greta turns to the young women. I am grateful to you, she says, for saving Ruth and Cheryl from being auctioned. I will always be grateful, but I would never have wanted you to compromise your virtue in doing so.

Oh, Mariche says. Mother. What virtue are you talking about? (She pronounces the word "virtue" as a hiss, a curse.) Virtue, she continues. My ass. You have your horses now. We all know that Neitje's and Autje's innocence was taken from them years ago. Let's be modern. (This is unexpected—and interesting. Being modern has not been an aspiration before, in the colony.) And Salome, you're behaving sanctimoniously and in bad faith if with one breath you push for this "freedom run" from the men of Molotschna and with the next breath pretend to be offended by the revolutionary (Not *revolutionary!* objects Greta) actions of the younger women in furthering our goal of leaving. Neitje and Autje used what was available to them to protect Ruth and Cheryl from auction, says Mariche. This isn't your personal catastrophe.

What are you talking about? asks Greta.

Mariche ignores her. She continues to address Salome. How do you suppose the bruises on my face, and Autje's, got there? Well, I will tell you. When Klaas went to get Ruth and Cheryl and discovered them missing he became very angry. He demanded I tell him where the horses were. I told him that while he was unconscious, getting his tooth pulled, the horses had broken out of the barn because somebody had forgotten to close the door. Klaas hit me and told me that was a lie, ridiculous. Ruth and Cheryl are never interested in running, he said. They're the laziest horses (Not true! says Greta) in Molotschna. He hit me again. Autje tried to intervene and Klaas slapped her face.

So, concludes Mariche. What of it? Can we proceed?

Agata pats Salome's hand.

Salome pulls it away and folds her arms.

Mariche has wounded Salome's pride. And Neitje has exposed her duplicity. She cannot be consoled.

We are wasting time, pleads Greta, by passing this burden, this sack of stones, from one to the next, by pushing our pain away. We mustn't do this. We mustn't play Hot Potato with our pain. Let's absorb it ourselves, each of us, she says. Let's inhale it, let's digest it, let's process it into fuel.

(This, I must confess, is a very loose translation. I'm pressed for time, and distracted because I'm remembering how Greta's late husband used to travel twelve miles south to purchase moonshine, get very drunk, and then have someone wrap him in a blanket and put him in his buggy, trusting that his horses would find their own way home, which they always did. Then Greta would roll her husband out of the blanket and put him to bed. I'm closer to understanding her deep love for Ruth and Cheryl, and I'm remembering Frint, his large eyes and long lashes, his velvet nose.)

Now somebody is climbing the ladder to the loft. It is Earnest Thiessen! He can barely walk let alone climb, and he is overexerting himself, smacking his lips, making grunting sounds.

Ona rushes to help him up the last few rungs.

Earnest asks us what we're doing here in his loft. Are you angels? he asks. Are you lost? Will you help me with my bath? He is gasping for air, but also laughing in fits and starts.

Ona helps him to sit down on a bale.

What are you bitches plotting? he asks the women (this in an even more archaic dialect of our archaic language).

Since becoming senile, Earnest Thiessen uses foul language regularly and the women are not alarmed. He was once a polite, reserved man, who, after working the fields all day, played tag in the dusky evening with his late wife, Annie, and their children, in their canola field, with kerosene lanterns to guide their chase.

Agata, also struggling for breath, gets up and walks to Earnest (they are cousins, the same age) and sits next to him on the bale.

Oh, Earnest, she says, we're getting old, aren't we?

Earnest puts his head on her shoulder and she smooths his wild, white hair. He asks if the women are devils.

No, says Agata, we're your friends.

He asks if the women are plotting to burn down his barn.

No, Ernie, says Agata, there's no plot, we're only women talking.

He seems to ponder this, then asks if Agata will help him with his bath.

Mejal offers to take Earnest back to his house and give him a washing. She will also pick up some bread and sausage from the summer kitchen, and feed Earnest, and bring the rest, as well as instant coffee, back to the loft for the women.

Will you make sure the water you use to wash Earnest is warm, but not hot, not scalding? asks Agata.

Mejal nods, and Earnest and Mejal slowly climb down the ladder.

Agata stands at the top of the ladder, her hands on her hips, watching. There is mint growing next to Earnest's front porch, she calls after them. You could pick some of it and add it to the warm water. Earnest would love that.

Agata goes to the window and watches for a long while, as Mejal and Earnest make their way back to Earnest's house. (I realize suddenly that she is saying goodbye to Earnest, it seems, for good.)

At last, she turns abruptly and addresses the other women. Is it agreed, she asks, that we will leave tonight after dark so that when we pass by the Chortiza and Hiakjeke colonies we won't be seen?

The women nod.

Ona asks Agata: But what about the colonies beyond Chortiza and Hiakjeke?

Agata frowns. What colonies? she asks.

That is exactly what I am asking, Ona replies. What colonies?

Well, says Agata, we don't know what lies beyond those colonies because we haven't travelled beyond them.

Mariche says: So we don't know if we won't be seen leaving because we don't know who else is there to see us?

That's right, says Agata. But we'll try to cover as much distance as we can while it's dark and then rest during the day, hidden.

Where will we hide? asks Greta. With our teams and our livestock and our little children and our chickens squawking incessantly and Grant reciting numbers constantly?

Greta, Agata says, impatiently, you know that we don't have the answers to these questions. We can't possibly know where we'll be hiding or who or what we'll encounter when we leave Molotschna. Let's not waste time by dwelling on the unknown.

But that's what thinking is, says Ona. And thinking is one of the things we want to be free to do. The things we know to exist or to be true don't require us to dwell on them.

Agata ignores Ona. What else do we have for our journey? she asks.

Well, Ona says, we must take animals, pigs and cows and chickens, to provide food along the way, and of course Ruth and Cheryl (Of course Ruth and Cheryl! echo the other women, facetiously), and the teams belonging to the other women.

Greta adds, We'll also need animal feed, and clean straw.

But who do those animals belong to? asks Mariche.

What difference does that make? Salome scoffs. We have to have animals with us to survive.

Mariche speaks up now. So, she says to Salome, you aren't morally opposed to doing what we must do to survive even if it means stealing?

(Ona and I exchange glances: Frint.)

Of course not, says Salome, and besides, the animals belong just as much to us as they do to the men.

Agreed, says Mariche. But then you shouldn't behave like a hypocrite when it comes to the other women doing what they feel they need to do in certain circumstances in order to survive.

Saving two old mares from auction by giving away your bodies to the semi-evolved (so, does Salome believe in evolution? I wonder) Koop brothers is not a question of survival, says Salome heatedly. Whereas having animals on hand when you're embarking on a long, unfamiliar journey to an unknown destination is definitely a question of survival. Have you ever heard of Noah and his ark?

Have *you* heard of Mary Magdalene and her friend Jesus, retorts Mariche.

Now Agata is laboriously getting to her feet once again. She enunciates every word, with venom in her voice. Now. I. Have. Heard. Enough! Are you women not aware that we are planning to run away tonight? That we are a large group, that the logistics are complicated, the variables multifold and the time fleeting! For the love of our Lord Jesus Christ and precious Saviour will you shut your pieholes, please!

Ona whispers: We're not *running* away, we're not rats fleeing a burning barn, we've made a decision to leave and—

Agata slams her hand on the table. Her other hand is on her heart. She collapses onto her feed pail/stool and does not speak.

Ona rushes to her mother. I'm sorry, she says. I promise I'll stay quiet. She removes her kerchief, dips it into the water barrel and places it on Agata's forehead. (Ona's hair cascades—this word retrieved from my memory of jailhouse literature, and I apologize—about her face and shoulders.)

The other women crowd around Agata. She smiles, eyes wide, nods her head, concentrates on her breathing.

All of us—the women and I—wait.

(Translator's note: There is no medicine for Agata in the colony, other than ether and the veterinarian spray, belladonna, used to knock out cows and horses—the same spray the attackers used on the girls and women of Molotschna.)

Greta prays.

Salome and Ona each hold one of Agata's hands and

synchronize their breathing. Mariche and the young women are quiet, looking on.

Agata has enough breath now to speak. *Yoma leid exhai*, she says. (This is untranslatable.)

The women laugh, relieved.

Where were we? she asks.

The women seem nervous about speaking now.

I raise my hand.

Please, says Agata, just speak already.

I explain that, since our meeting ended yesterday, I have managed to procure the safe from the co-op, a stick of dynamite and a world map. (After leaving Ona on the wash house roof last evening I felt emboldened, brave, for reasons having to do with not sleeping, plus pure joy, the sweet memory of our conversation, our proximity, alive inside me.)

And a sextant, I add. However, I'm not sure that will be useful.

A sextant! says Ona. She smiles. To measure angles?

I shrug.

The women, other than Salome, seem startled. They look at me.

Greta's arms go up over her head. Amen, she says.

Mariche asks: What do you mean, when you say you have dynamite?

To blow up the safe, says Salome. To get our money.

Ona asks, What will happen when the men return to find the safe missing?

We can blame it on the Koop brothers, says Salome.

The others ignore her.

Perhaps we will be able to leave a ten percent tithe of the money behind for the church, suggests Autje.

Salome snorts.

It was a serious suggestion, says Autje.

Where did you find dynamite? asks Mariche. She is squinting at me through the damaged soft tissue of her face.

I explain that it's used by the colony men to scare the alligators out of the north lagoon. I have encased it in pigskin, like a sausage, I tell the women, so it won't be detected.

But won't the dynamite blow the money that is inside the safe to pieces as well? Mariche asks.

I hadn't thought of that, I admit. It might be easier to have someone decode the lock.

Yes, says Salome, but who? Remember, we will be in hiding in the countryside, not strolling about some city with countless decoding businesses lining the streets.

That's a good point, says Agata. I don't imagine that on some desolate dirt trail we'll bump into an individual advertising his business for decoding safes.

True, says Greta. He would be an unsuccessful businessman if that were the case.

Though, adds Ona, not necessarily an unsuccessful decoder.

Right, says Agata. To be continued. She smiles, moves her upper body back and forth. Says: We know that the city is approximately seven hours to the south of us by team and buggy at a quick clip. Longer in the spring when the coulee floods.

We do? asks Ona.

This is the prevailing wisdom from the men who have spoken of the journey, explains Agata. (Salome, under her breath: Oh well, yes, wisdom.) But, continues Agata, we're not going to the city.

Right, says Greta, definitely not the city. She regales the women with a spontaneous story about a flush toilet from the city (I gather that Greta, surprisingly, has been to the city at least once in her life, although I don't know the circumstances): how she pushed the handle down and, as a result of the loud, engulfing noise it made, leapt away from the toilet as though it were a grenade and she had just pulled the pin.

Greta, says Agata, why are you stalling?

I don't know, admits Greta. She amends that: I'm nervous.

We're all nervous, says Agata. We can't avoid nervousness.

(I glance up at Ona, who is returning her hair to its kerchief. A black bobby pin pokes out from the corner of her mouth. The underside of her arm, as she reaches for her hair, is very smooth and white, like the keel of a new canoe.)

Agata continues: We will want to find water and perhaps some grazing land for our animals, and we will want to cross borders.

But which ones? asks Mariche.

The women are quiet.

I speak again: I have wrapped the map around a large block of cheese and covered it with ordinary brown paper. The safe is in the back of Greta's buggy, under the back seat, ready to go. I also packed some onions and some soap and pieces of wood for traction if the wheels get mired in mud or for kindling to start a fire. (I glance at Ona. She is pleased with me, I believe.)

And the dynamite and the map? Ona asks. The peculiar sausage and the cheese?

They're also in Greta's buggy, I say. In the hatbox at the front.

Have Ruth and Cheryl been brought back to Greta's barn? Agata asks.

Yes, says Neitje, we got them early this morning from the Koop—

Good, yes, yes, interrupts Agata. Let's not return to that subject.

Ona expresses concern that I will get into trouble, that I will be found guilty through association. Klaas now knows that you have been with the women, in the loft, ostensibly learning how to sew, she says. With the women and the safe having vanished, August will be blamed. Who else would know where the key was? Surely, not any of the women. August will be judged to be the instigator. How can we be sure August won't be found guilty and punished by Peters? Or excommunicated?

(I am touched by Ona's concern for me. I don't care about any of those things, about being found guilty—I am guilty—or about being evicted from the colony. If Ona isn't here, why should I be?)

But the map, says Salome, changing the subject, to my relief. We can't read it.

Neitje asks her mother if she's heard the news.

What news? answers Salome.

North. East. West. South, says Neitje.

Agata smiles and nods approvingly, yet again moving her body to the left and right. The others purse their lips and shake their heads.

I venture to speak once again. I tell the women that I've created a legend.

The women smile politely, waiting for an explanation.

For the map, I say. I explain that I've drawn asterisks on the map that coincide with pictures in the legend.

There is silence.

I drew them, I say again, stupidly.

Like Michelangelo, says Ona, with a half smile at me.

Do you know your numbers? I ask the women. I'm deeply ashamed to be asking them this.

We do, yes, says Greta. Of course we do.

Do we? asks Mariche.

The girls do, adds Greta.

Autje and Neitje nod in agreement.

Agata explains: August, she says, we know how to write our names. That's all. And it takes me longer to write my name than to plant a crop of canola.

Greta laughs. And to harvest it the next fall, she says.

Mariche says that she doesn't actually know how to write her name, she's been too busy to learn.

I will help you later, offers Ona. When we have more time.

Mariche pauses, considers, then bows her head regally. I accept, she says.

So what do the pictures show? Ona asks me.

Rivers, roads big and small, towns and cities and borders, train tracks, I say. It's only a map of this part of the world, this celestial sphere.

It's a map of the heavens? asks Mariche.

It's a map of the Americas, I say.

Mariche, scornfully: Then why do you say "celestial sphere"?

Ona asks me: What direction do you think we should take?

Before I can respond, there is a commotion on the ladder.

Mejal has returned with food, but she is agitated. She has heard that there is a fire raging north of the colony and there is talk that the men in the city will be coming back early to save their animals.

Shall we assume they'll save us as well? says Ona.

The older women laugh raucously, though briefly, at this. Agata stops to catch her breath.

We'll head out, then, says Mariche. We should go. She abruptly stands up.

Now the others are rising up from their pails as well.

We were going to leave when it got dark, protests Greta.

We don't have time to wait, says Mariche. She turns to Mejal. Who told you about the fire?

Mejal is reluctant to say who it was.

The Koop brothers? asks Autje.

Mejal nods.

What are the Koop brothers doing in Molotschna? Salome asks.

Mejal shrugs.

Well, I don't believe what the Koop brothers are saying about a fire, Salome says. I think they are calling our bluff, aware of something going on, forcing our hand, so that we will make a move, leave early and be caught. They want to be heroes, says Salome. They want to be kings. Do you smell smoke? Are the skies dark? Are the animals jumpy? Are the flies still? Are the birds making a fuss? Are Mejal's allergies unruly? No, she answers her own questions. No to everything. There is no fire.

Mariche turns to Autje. Were you and Neitje aware that the Koop boys were in Molotschna? she asks.

Autje and Neitje won't answer. They look away, frightened.

Don't tell me you told them we were planning to leave, says Salome. What on earth is the matter with you?

Autje begins to cry.

It was a mistake, Neitje says. The Koop brothers gave us mistletoe vodka, and we were excited. We felt so brave. We're very sorry. Very sorry.

Autje, through tears, says, It's impossible for the Koop boys to inform on us. There is no way they can reach the men in the city on time, not if it's seven hours each way at a fast clip.

I have heard some of the men in Chortiza are in possession of telephones, states Mejal.

But not the Koop brothers, says Neitje. They would have shown us if they'd had them.

I clear my throat. Even if the Koop brothers were to have telephones, I say, there is no signal here. They'd have to go to the top of Zweibach Hill to get a signal.

What are you talking about, August? asks Agata. What kind of signal?

Before I can answer, Mejal points out this isn't a problem anyway, because the men of Molotschna have no telephones from which to receive a call.

I raise my hand again and speak: Peters does.

What? No! says Greta.

Peters has had a phone for years, I explain. He plays games with it while the other men are working in the field.

But still, says Agata, you say the Koop brothers, if they had a telephone, would have to climb Zweibach Hill?

Ona is holding her stomach, pale.

Greta prays. Agata thinks.

Neitje raises her voice, insists: They don't have telephones! They would have bragged about them if they did.

The women nod, trusting this.

Agata says, So, the Koop boys are waiting for us to make our move and then will ride to the city to inform the men that we've left, or will perhaps themselves prevent us from leaving. By claiming there is a fire to the north of Molotschna they think they can force us to move southwards, towards the city where the men are, a trap.

Well, says Ona, that would seal our fate.

Obviously, we'll disregard the fire nonsense, says Mariche. The animals would tell us if that were true. We'll head north, away from the men.

But the Koop brothers might prevent us from leaving in the first place, says Greta.

That's impossible, says Salome. How can those two scrawny shit for brains prevent all of us women from leaving.

They have guns, says Mejal. They have horse whips.

Well, so do we, says Salome.

No, Agata says, we certainly do not. We have no guns and whips. Well, we have buggy whips, but we're not about to start whipping people.

Greta mentions that she's never even whipped Ruth or Cheryl, and they are horses.

Agata frowns at her, fed up. If it wasn't for the safety of Ruth and Cheryl, Autje and Neitje wouldn't have had to agree to demeaning themselves for the pleasure of the Koop brothers and the Koop brothers wouldn't have fed mistletoe vodka to Autje and Neitje, and Autje and Neitje wouldn't have let slip, due to being inebriated, that the women were planning to leave Molotschna.

Salome says that she can get some guns. Or even better, she says, August could get some guns for us. After all, he was able to procure dynamite. Can you? she asks me.

I'm tongue-tied. I tear at my head, hair comes away.

No, says Agata once again. We won't have guns and whips.

I have another concern, Mariche says. The Koop boys might rally the men of Chortiza and Hiakjeke to help them stop us from leaving.

Greta scoffs at this. The men of Chortiza and Hiakjeke, she says, aren't interested in the women of Molotschna, only their own. They would consider it a victory over the men of Molotschna if we left. They'd gloat for generations.

The women nod in unison, solemnly.

Why are the Koop boys from Chortiza so interested in preventing the women from Molotschna from leaving in the first place? Salome asks. What difference does it make to them? She directs her gaze at Neitje and Autje.

Neitje says: Because they want to marry us.

Salome rises from her pail. You will not marry a Koop boy, or any Chortizer, period, she says to Neitje.

Autje, defensively: The boys and girls of Chortiza have been forbidden to marry each other for five years to weed out the deformed babies. So the Chortiza boys are going to Molotschna and Hiakjeke to find wives. That's what the Koop boys told us.

I'll marry whomever I want, says Neitje.

Salome's nostrils flare. So, she says, the men of Chortiza and Hiakjeke are interested in the women of Molotschna after all. We mustn't let them see us leave. The city is south of Molotschna. Chortiza is west and Hiakjeke is east. We'll go north.

Nettie/Melvin has climbed the ladder now and is in the loft. She is silent, standing before the women. Agata begs her to speak, to give us the news from the ground.

Nettie stares at the window and speaks: The little children (she uses the word *kjinja*) are ready. They are clean. Their extra clothing is in barrels. Their linen is in barrels. Their boots are in barrels. Their hats are in boxes. They are fed.

Thank you, Melvin, Agata says. Melvin smiles for the first time in one hundred years at this, the first appellation of her new name. She smiles at the open window, a silent communion with the sunlight of Molotschna, now hers.

Greta asks Melvin if Cornelius is also ready and if his wheelchair has been packed away? Cornelius will not be joining us after all, Melvin answers to the window. His mother is in the Do Nothing camp, and Cornelius has no choice but to stay with her.

Autje and Neitje frown and moan. All the youth of Molotschna, particularly the girls, are taken with Cornelius, with his jokes and comedies and creativity. Cornelius and his mother may yet change their minds, Agata reassures the young women. Perhaps they will join us elsewhere.

No, says Mariche. That's not accurate, that won't be possible. When the men return, no women will be allowed to leave.

She turns to Autje and Neitje. You will see Cornelius in heaven one day, she says, and he will be able to walk. He will run into your arms.

The young women nod, tentatively. (I surmise that holding Cornelius in their arms is not exactly what they had in mind.)

Agata places her hands on the table, for support. Melvin, she asks, are you, too, ready for the journey?

Melvin doesn't answer. The women wait.

No, Melvin says at last. I am not ready.

The women make noises of alarm, and some look about to speak.

Then Melvin says: But I am coming with you.

The women smile and sigh with relief. Greta says, Yes, who of us can say we're ready, after all?

I can, says Salome.

Melvin, Agata says. Please return to the children and wait with them in the fallow field next to the school.

She instructs Melvin to engage the children in some type of play, perhaps Flying Dutchmen, and to keep an eye on the cow path that runs along the field. That is where the other women will find them, on their way out of Molotschna. We will have at least ten buggies and ten teams, Agata says.

Including Ruth and Cheryl, adds Greta.

Goddammit, Mother, please, says Mariche. (Ona and I exchange the slightest of glances. I imagine she is as startled by this outburst as I am. But Greta simply closes her eyes briefly and dips her chin.)

The strongest of us, says Agata, will walk alongside the buggies with the other animals, including the yearlings who will serve as pack mules, and with the children if they are restless and prefer to skip ahead.

Ona smiles at this, repeats the words: Skip ahead.

Melvin nods. Then she says to Salome: Aaron, your son, is missing.

Salome looks at Melvin, at the other women. She stands. What? she says. What do you mean?

He didn't come to the summer kitchen for lunch with the other children, Melvin says.

But that doesn't mean he's missing, says Salome. She walks to the window. I asked Aaron to get the teams ready, she tells us, to water the horses, to pick the burrs from their saddle blankets and to clean their hooves. So he must be in a barn, she says. He's not missing.

Melvin speaks to the window.

I can't hear what she is saying.

Salome takes Melvin's arm. Speak to me directly, she insists. Not to the window. Please. I won't harm you. I am not your enemy!

But Melvin is frightened of Salome and backs away.

You must calm down, Agata tells Salome. She turns to Melvin. You are safe, she says. Aaron will be found.

But we're leaving now, soon, says Salome. I'm not leaving without him.

As if she can't help herself, Mariche points out that one moment ago Salome was insisting she was ready to go.

We are all leaving people behind, says Mariche. It's sad, it's difficult, why should Salome be given special allowance to throw a tantrum about it?

Salome is climbing down the ladder.

Melvin whispers, again to the window. Some of the children told me that Aaron didn't want to go, she says, that he felt stupid leaving with the little children and the women.

Salome has reached the bottom of the ladder, and is on the barn floor. She jumped down from a middle rung. We hear a thud.

Salome, calls Agata. Come back!

Ona calls down to Salome. Aaron will be found, she says. He will leave with us after all, surely.

Melvin is still at the window, speaking. She tells us that Salome is running now, her skirts are flying behind her, she is bent into the wind, kicking up dust.

We must remain calm, Agata beseeches the women. Salome will return, she says. She will find Aaron and convince him to leave. Melvin, go now to the other children and bring them to the field to play games.

But what if she doesn't convince Aaron? asks Ona. She won't leave with us if he doesn't also leave. What will happen to Miep?

Agata nods. We have problems, she concedes. Let me think.

Ona says, Perhaps Salome will allow me to take Miep, to be her temporary guardian.

My words are blurring on the page.

The women are speaking too quickly for me to keep up. They are planning. Lists are useless to us, Agata tells me, but still I must keep up and make as many lists as I can, and the older boys, like Aaron presumably, if he is found, and if he accompanies the women, will be able to read them to the women.

Lists of what? I ask Agata.

Of good things, she says, of memories, of plans. Whatever you feel goes into a good list, please write it down. She laughs. (I notice that beneath her laugh, her breathing is choppy, laboured.)

Thank you for your efforts, August, she says. John and Monica (these are the names of my parents, excommunicated many years ago, deceased, missing. These are long stories, but familiar to Molotschnans) would be so proud of you. God bless you.

Tears are streaming down my face. Yes, I will make a list.

The women rise, ready to leave the loft.

Agata is breathing heavily and Ona looks at her with

concern. Mother, she says, this will be an arduous trip, perilous.

Agata laughs. I'm aware of that, she says.

Today is the day that the Lord hath made, she adds. Let us rejoice and be glad in it!

Then, to Ona, she says softly: I won't be buried in Molotschna. Help me into a buggy now and I'll die on the trail.

Ona laughs, but her eyes tear up.

I can hardly write.

The women help each other down the ladder, in a chain.

What about August? says Ona. (Note: these are the last words I hear her speak.)

I smile, stammer, wave. I am ridiculous.

Agata is the last to climb down. I rise to my feet.

Agata turns to me and smiles. August, she says, wouldn't you marry my Ona?

I return Agata's smile. I've longed for nothing else, I say. I have asked Ona many times over the years, asked for her hand.

And she always said no? asks Agata.

I smile again, call out to Ona: One last fact for you, Ona, I say . . . I will always love you!

I hear Ona laughing, but I can no longer see her. She is leaving.

Agata is climbing down, is almost at the bottom of the ladder.

And she loves you, too, August, says Agata. She catches her breath. She loves everyone.

How will I live without these women?

My heart will stop.

I will try to teach the boys about Ona. She will be my Polaris, my Crux, my north and south and east and west, my news, my direction, my map and my explosives, my rifle. I will write Ona's name at the top of every lesson guide. I imagine schoolhouses in all the Mennonite colonies in all the world, as the sun is disappearing, stealing away to share its warmth and light with other parts of the world, and everything belongs to everyone, and it's time for the chores and for dinner and for praying and sleeping, and the children beg their teacher for one more story about Ona, who began as the devil's daughter and became God's most precious child. The soul of Molotschna.

And the gates of hell shall not prevail against her.

When the elders and bishops of the Mennonite colonies preach the story of Saul and his conversion, they will at the same time repeat and invoke and incant the story of Ona, with her messy hair and filthy hem and easy laugh and love of facts (dragonflies have six legs but can't walk!) which, to her and maybe to all Molotschnans, are like dreams, when a man's dream becomes for us the truth, when Menno Simons' fevered vision is the word, when Peters' angry interpretation is our narrow path and facts are in the world, the world we don't belong in, or can't belong in, or perhaps do belong in, and they are kept from us and the real facts take on mythical importance, awe, they are gifts, samizdat, currency, they are the Eucharist, blood, forbidden, and imagine this: a fetus can help to repair his mother's damaged heart, or any organ, the brain even, by sending stem cells to the organ; and listen to this: the hearts of two women who suffered from heart weakness were later found to contain cells derived from the cells of male fetuses years after they gave birth to their sons . . . and so I invoke Ona's love of precision but also of mysterious rivers and secret playing, and her embrace and her kindness and her unborn child and repa‐ration and disturbing dreams, and her love of myth, of madness, of skipping ahead, of listening and solitude and fists raised to constellations, of rooftops and wash houses and shining eyes, eyes that shine as the story takes hold and cruelty becomes a weak flame, then is gone.

Agata reaches up and pats my knee. I'm towering over her now, and I bend to touch her shoulder. She is descending, she puts her hand on mine. I remind her to hang on to the ladder with both hands.

She asks me to stay in the loft and to wait for Salome, who will return here in search of the women.

Tell her, says Agata, that we are gathering behind the schoolhouse.

What about Aaron? I say.

There is no response. The women have left the loft.

The list, as requested by Agata.

Sun.

Stars.

Pails.

Birth.

The harvest.

Numbers.

Sounds.

Window.

Straw.

Frint.

Beams.

Futility.

My mother.

My father.

Language.

Soft tissue. (Its resilience and ability to remodel even as it protects the hard tissue, the rigid endoskeleton of the human body. A colony. Often defined by what it is not. I can hear Mariche's voice, mocking: Why do you talk that way, August?)

A dream. (About small houses built of stones, easily dismantled overnight and carried off in wagons, to be rebuilt elsewhere, and then again dismantled, and in each dismantling the chalky substance of the stone erodes a little bit more until the house is so small that it's not a house anymore. In my dream, Ona was put in charge of these houses and seemed always to be engaged in a public debate about whether the houses should be restored, preserved or allowed to erode to dust, as is their nature. If the houses are made to be dismantled, impermanent, and if by dismantling the houses time and time again they erode into dust, then mustn't we let them? That's what they're made to do. If we don't want our houses to erode then we must, in the first place, make them in a different way. But surely we can't preserve houses that were built to disappear. Some people attending this public debate, in my dream, disagreed with Ona. They said: But it's a question of heritage, or of a heritage site, an artifact and a physical reminder of what once was. And Ona would say, in my dream, smiling, Ah, but that's something else!)

Flies.

Manure.

Wind.

Women.

My list is listing, listless. The origin: *liste*, from Middle
English, meaning desire. Which is also the origin of the
word "listen."

But now I hear voices, and clambering on the ladder.

The young women, Autje and Neitje, appear in the
loft. They are surprised to see me. Hide, quickly, they say.

August Epp, After the Meeting

WHILE I HID IN A HAY BALE:

The Koop brothers came to the loft. Their voices low, male, nervous, surprising. Autje and Neitje spoke with the boys, softly, laughing, stretches of breathing. I couldn't hear well from inside the bale, straw in my ears. The boys and the girls lay down with each other in a corner of the loft, across from where I hid, beneath the lowest rafters. They kissed. The girls laughed. They murmured. Told the boys to close their eyes. Then it was silent. I couldn't hear. I couldn't see. Then I heard a familiar voice. It was Salome.

I heard footsteps coming towards me. The straw was brushed away from my face. I saw Salome!

She told me to get out of the bale.

I climbed out of the bale on my hands and knees, afraid of what I would see.

Autje and Neitje were standing beside Salome, watching me. They pulled straw from their hair. It was loose, wild. Their kerchiefs were tied around their wrists, stylishly, their white socks rolled down around their ankles. Behind them lay the Koop brothers, asleep or dead, not moving. I looked at Salome for an answer.

She told me she had made them unconscious with the belladonna spray. She told me that she had instructed the girls, Autje and Neitje, to lure the Koop brothers to the loft with promises of intimacy, to make a considerable amount of noise so that she could enter the loft undetected. She told me that now the Koop brothers would not be able to go to the city to inform on the women.

She told the girls to go to the buggies waiting behind the schoolhouse. It was time to leave.

The girls waved goodbye to me, diffidently. Goodbye, Mr. Epp, they said, over their shoulders. They climbed down the ladder, then ran laughing, exuberantly, away from the barn, away from Molotschna.

But where is Aaron? I asked Salome.

She told me that she had found him, that he was already in the buggy, waiting.

You convinced him to leave? I asked her.

No, she said, I didn't. I used the spray on him too.

My eyes widened. I began to speak.

I had to, said Salome, he can't stay here. It's just as though I had picked up a sleeping child in the night and carried him away from a house that was on fire.

Is it? I asked. What if he changes his mind?

Salome shook her head. It will be too late, she said, we will be gone. He's coming with me. He's my child.

I nodded. She told me she had sprayed Scarface Janz also.

I had to, she said again. She was planning to go to the city to tell the men.

But does she know how to get there? I asked her.

No, said Salome, of course not.

Then it was an idle threat, I said. There was no need to spray her.

But I was afraid, said Salome, our warrior, our captain.

I wanted to tell her that if Aaron were to run away from Salome again, to return to Molotschna, that I would keep an eye on him. I would walk beside him, as we have learned to say.

But Salome was leaving. She asked me, rather, to keep an eye on the Koop brothers. To make sure they remained unconscious for seven or eight hours, long enough for the women to get away from Molotschna. She handed me a container that held the belladonna spray.

Use it on them again if they wake up too soon, she said. But don't let the elders find you with this in your possession. She laughed.

Where did you find it? I asked her.

She told me it had always been stored in Peters' dairy barn.

Peters' barn? I asked. (Is it for good or for evil that Peters is the caretaker of the belladonna spray?)

Salome had turned and was walking towards the ladder.

Goodbye, August, she said.

I asked her to wait. I went to her. I put my hand on the fleshy part of her arm, above her elbow. She didn't flinch. She held my gaze.

Please take care of Ona and her baby, I said.

Salome nodded, promised that she would. Ona was her sister, her blood, and the baby too.

She began to climb down. We really have to hurry, she said.

But you're not fleeing, I said. You're not rats running from a burning building. She laughed again.

That's right, she said. We've chosen to leave.

But not Aaron, I wanted to say. Salome, I said.

What now, August? Haven't you noticed how determined I am to go? She laughed.

Don't come back, I said. Don't ever come back, any of you.

She laughed again. She nodded, and told me she'd miss me, to be a good teacher, and that I had straw in my hair.

Oh! Wait! I told her.

August! she said, exasperated.

I ran to the table, the piece of plywood, and picked up my notebooks, the minutes, and ran back to the ladder.

Please give these to Ona, I said.

But you know she can't read them, said Salome. What will she do with them? Use them as kindling?

Her child will read them, I said. Tell her to keep them, not to use them as kindling.

Salome laughed once again. I hadn't realized how much she laughed, like her mother, like all the women of Molotschna. Saving their breath for laughter.

Unless we have nothing else to start a fire, Salome said.

Yes, I said, unless that is the case. And I thought: For kindling, for warmth, the minutes would give life to the women as the women had given life to me. The words were futile, a document. Life was the only thing. Migration, movement, freedom. We want to protect our children and we want to think. We want to keep our faith. We want the world. Do we want the world? If I'm outside it, my life outside it, outside of my life, if my life isn't in the world, then what good is it? To teach? To teach what, if not the world?

For a brief moment I wondered if the Koop brothers had been telling the truth, if there really was a fire raging to the north of Molotschna. Perhaps it was possible for them to get wind of this before the animals, to know something the animals hadn't yet sensed. If the fire is in the north and the men are in the south, in the city, and the prying eyes of the Chortiza and Hiakjeke colonies to the west and east, then where will the women go?

But surely there can't be a fire to the north. And now I must wait for the Koop boys to regain consciousness to find out whether it's true or not.

We'll meet again, I said to Salome—our traditional farewell.

We'll meet again, she said to me.

Salome took the notebooks. She descended the ladder.

I went to the window and watched her running away from the barn. I could just catch a glimpse of the convoy of buggies lining up behind the schoolhouse.

While waiting for the Koop brothers to wake up:

I had planned to leave also, after the women left. I had planned to finally kill myself. Instead, I find myself watching over the Koop boys, making sure they remain unconscious long enough for the women to gain sufficient ground.

Moments ago, I sprayed a small amount of the belladonna in the face of one of the Koop boys, the larger one
named Joren—or is he Sibbe? This larger of the two Koop
boys was calling out in his sleep and moving his legs as
though preparing to stand up. He is quiet now.

Both the boys are breathing regularly, deeply, their
colour is good, robust, and their pulses are even. I have
moved them both onto their sides so they won't choke if
they vomit. I have elevated and cushioned their heads
slightly, by bunching up straw beneath them. Their hands,
calloused and strong, are clasped in prayer position, the
tips of their fingers grazing their chins. It is clear that neither of the boys has ever used a razor. They are facing
each other, though oblivious of course, and in such close
proximity their resemblance as brothers is striking.
Perhaps they're twins? Although the one, Joren, or Sibbe,
is definitely larger than the other, taller and more muscular. His feet are bigger, at least by the look of his cowboy
boots. Joren, let's say, had undone his belt buckle and
several of the buttons on his pants. I fixed that, redid his
buttons and belt buckle. And Sibbe's shirttail had become
untucked. I fixed that also.

What a quiet loft. The women are gone. I stood at
the window and watched them leave. I thought: I have
come to Molotschna as a last resort, for peace and to find
my purpose, and the women have left Molotschna for the
same reasons.

There was some commotion at the front of the convoy, just before they began to move. One of the horses,
likely neither Ruth nor Cheryl, who are too old and

circumspect to act out, had reared up and shifted the axle on the buggy to a right angle, making it impossible to move forward. The axle had to be realigned and the horse made calm. But that passed and the teams and the buggies fell into formation, at least twelve of them or more, filled with women and children and supplies. They were far off, at least two hundred metres, and I wasn't able to make out faces or individual forms.

At first, I thought I heard the women singing but then I corrected myself, knowing that the women wouldn't do anything to call attention to themselves in this moment, or possibly ever. It was only the wind making a whistling sound in the long grass outside Earnest Thiessen's barn, not singing, not Ona's clear, high soprano soaring. Or it was singing, but I was only imagining it, or remembering it.

I stood at the window. Had a face peered out from around the front barrier of the fourth buggy in the convoy, and a hand lifted in farewell?

I have a gun. I've had it all along. When Salome—or was it Mariche?—asked if the women had guns, I could have offered to give it to them, but I remained silent. Selfish. Why is there no word in our dying language for salvation? I wish I had given the gun to them. Agata and Greta and Ona and the younger women would have refused to take it but Salome, likely, or Mejal, or even Mariche, might have been convinced.

Two days ago when I met Ona on the dirt path that runs between her house and the shed where I sleep I also had the gun with me, in my hand. The shadows were lengthening and we kept side-stepping into sunlight as we spoke, as I mentioned earlier, when I had wanted to ask, but failed to, if Ona considered me to be a physical reminder of evil. I had been crying, again, wandering around the fields outside Molotschna, determined that day to shoot myself. When I saw Ona on the path, I considered running off, or throwing the gun into the cornfield, but instead I froze and simply stared at her as she approached.

She was smiling, almost skipping as she came near, and waving too. When we were face to face she asked me where I was going, what I was doing, and I told her nowhere, and nothing. She asked me if I was going hunting. I said no, not hunting. I glanced at the gun and said, oh, this, and mentioned that I was returning it to the co-op.

But why do you have it? she asked me.

I looked into her eyes and held my gaze. She stopped smiling. We were silent.

She started to speak but then stopped. I hung my head. I didn't want her to see me crying yet again. She took my hand and we made our first step towards the sunlight, outside the shadow that had formed around us. She put my hand on her pregnant belly and told me, as though she had been able to read my mind, that she had prayed for me, she had prayed that I would find God's grace, and that I was a physical reminder of goodness and of hope, and of life after violence. She was referring to my mother, and to my father—not the man who raised me and then disappeared, but to Peters, the younger.

My father wasn't excommunicated because he showed colonists photographs of paintings by Michelangelo, or my mother because she ran a secret school for girls in the barn, during milking. We were sent away because by the age of twelve, as I approached the brink of adulthood, I bore a remarkable resemblance to Peters and I had become a symbol, in the colony, or at least to Peters, of shame and violence and unacknowledged sin and of the failure of the Mennonite experiment.

Was that true? Could it be? Where is evil? In the world outside or the world inside? On the serene surface of the Black Sea or in the mysterious river that runs beneath it, that preserves everything, but only because there is no air, no breath. No movement. No life.

When I was a boy in England, my mother was given a job at a library. We were alone. My father had left; he had driven himself to the airport and left the car in a parking lot. He hadn't fallen asleep for a thousand years. He had boarded a plane.

My mother took books home from the library. Books come home and home again, and fathers fly away. My mother explained to me that a French writer, Flaubert, who was once "Flobert," wrote a story at the age of fifteen called "Rage and Impotence." She read it to me in French and then in English, both broken, filled with pauses, if pauses can be filling, because neither one was her language, the dead language that she and I used to share secrets . . . Flaubert dreamed of love in a tomb. But the dream evaporated and the tomb remained. That was Flaubert's story and perhaps, too, the story of the Mennonites of Molotschna.

It's funny now—or was then, too, but I didn't see it—to think of how I recited (Oh, why do I use the word "recited," so top-heavy, so comical), how I *repeated* those words to my cellmates, the words of Flaubert, wrapped in the memory of my mother, of love and death, the death of a dream, or perhaps not death. A part of my scalp was removed, brutally, when I finished, the part that I scratch at wildly, as though I'm searching for the source of something, something I've lost, a frenzy of pain. Why does the mention of love, the memory of love, the memory of love lost, the promise of love, the end of love, the absence of love, the burning, burning need for love, need to love, result in so much violence?

Molotschna.

Ona held my hand to her belly until I felt the life inside her and I smiled. Why has Peters allowed me back into the colony? Why did the librarian suggest that I return to Molotschna? The women in the loft have taught me that consciousness is resistance, that faith is action, that time is running out. But can faith also be to return, to stay, to serve?

Much service, too, does he who turns his plough, and again breaks crosswise through the ridges he raised.

Is there a small but vital, burning piece of Peters that is seeking to make peace? And mustn't I acknowledge that? Or even if it isn't a vital, burning piece of Peters but a barely glowing ember, mustn't I hope that it will grow? In which case, mustn't I be here, in Molotschna, as a physical reminder not of evil, but of God's grace?

I don't know. I only know one fact: that I'm of more use being alive and teaching basic reading, writing and math, and organizing games of Flying Dutchmen, than lying dead in a field with a bullet in my brain. Ona knew that all along. She told me she had a favour to ask of me, that she needed me to take the minutes for the women's meetings. I hesitated at first, but what excuse could I make? What could I tell her? That unfortunately I wouldn't be available to take the minutes because I'd be fatally wounded from a self-inflicted gunshot to my head?

I understand now that I had told her exactly this, with my eyes, with my silence, with the gun. (Especially with the gun.)

I asked her what good the minutes would do her and the other women if they were unable to read them? (But she may well have asked me instead, What good is it to be alive if you are not in the world?)

And that's when she told me the story of the squirrel and the rabbit and of their secret playing, and said that perhaps she hadn't been meant to see them playing—yet she *had* seen them. Maybe there was no reason for the women to *have* minutes they couldn't read. The purpose, all along, was for me to *take* them.

The purpose was for me to take them, the minutes. Life.

I smile. I see the world turning in on itself, like waves, but without a sea or shore to contain them. There was no point to the minutes. I have to laugh.

I stand at the window and sniff the air for any sign of smoke, but there is none, or if there is, I can't detect it.

Are the women rushing headlong into a raging fire?

I look at the boys, asleep, unconscious to be exact, and plead silently with them to tell me the truth.

ACKNOWLEDGEMENTS

My gratitude belongs to three women without whom these pages would be blank: my editor, Lynn Henry; my agent, Sarah Chalfant; and my mother, Elvira Toews.

I wish, also, to acknowledge the girls and women living in patriarchal, authoritarian (Mennonite and non-Mennonite) communities across the globe. Love and solidarity.

A NOTE ON THE AUTHOR

MIRIAM TOEWS' most recent novel, the bestselling *All My Puny Sorrows*, was published in 2014 to wide acclaim. It won the Rogers Writers' Trust Fiction Prize and the Canadian Authors Association Award for Fiction, and was shortlisted for the Scotiabank Giller Prize, the Folio Prize and the Wellcome Book Prize, among other accolades. Toews is the author of five other bestselling and acclaimed novels—*Summer of My Amazing Luck*, *A Boy of Good Breeding*, *A Complicated Kindness* (winner of the Governor General's Literary Award for Fiction, winner of Canada Reads, and a finalist for the Scotiabank Giller Prize), *The Flying Troutmans* and *Irma Voth*—and one work of non-fiction, *Swing Low: A Life*. She has also won the Libris Award for Fiction Book of the Year, the Writers' Trust Marian Engel/Timothy Findley Award, and Italy's Sinbad Award for Fiction. Miriam Toews lives in Toronto.